W9-BVU-682

CONTENT ADVISORY:

THIS GRAPHIC NOVEL CONTAINS INSTANCES OF DEAD NAMING, HOMOPHOBIA, TRANSPHOBIA, MISGENDERING, AND FORCED GENDER EXPRESSION THAT MAY BE DISTRESSING TO SOME.

ISBN 978-1-338-77552-5 (PB)

ISBN 978-1-338-72553-2 (HC)

10 9 8 7 6 5 4 3 2 1   21 22 23 24 25

Printed in China   62

First edition, November 2021

Edited by Michael Petranek and Lori Wieczorek

Book design by Jeff Shake, Salena Mahina, and Cheung Tai

Lettering by Dezi Sienty

For Tapas:

Edited by Brooke Huang

Colored by Dojo Gubser

Art assistance by Sera Swati

Additional assistance by Selena Ahmed

Editor in Chief Michael Son

Dear Reader,

Magical Boy is a story I've been wanting to tell for a long time. I wanted to create a story about a hero who embarks on a messy, funny, difficult, outrageous, and ultimately rewarding journey, and I wanted that hero to be someone who all readers—but especially transmen—can cheer on and relate to.

Like any good story, there will be conflict. There will be times when Max faces hardships and obstacles to his transition, and some of those will be from Max's own internal struggles as well. He's a teen who's still going through the messy process of figuring out who he is as a person in many aspects. There are people in his life who won't understand him, and there will be times when he doubts himself.

I know that *Magical Boy* will be tough for some to read at times. I wanted to create a story that is authentic and true to experiences that many transmen have faced, but please don't doubt that I have the best intentions for Max. I know that *Magical Boy* can't be representative of every transman's experience, but I hope that you'll find his journey of self-discovery and overcoming the fictional obstacle of his Magical Girl lineage to be fun, compelling, and genuine.

Max is a character that I hold close to my heart, and I hope that you'll hold him close to yours, too.

—The Kao

Episode 1:
IT'S MAX

SIIIGGHHHHH

SHE'S DOING IT AGAIN.
TWITCH TWITCH

Happy Birthday Aine
♡Mom

TOSS
PTHH
THIS ISN'T ME.

MEOW.
MUUUCH BETTER.
MEOW.

OOF.
WHAT DO YOU THINK, WALNUT?
JUST LOOK AT IT.
YOU'D THINK AFTER ALL THE YEARS SHE'D KNOW
...I DON'T WEAR THIS STUFF!
GURGLE
!
BLEH
SPLAT

MY BED!
...
RUB
RUB
RUB
MORNING, BIRTHDAY GIRL!
!

...
WHY AREN'T YOU WEARING THE DRESS I BOUGHT YOU?!
UHHH!
WALNUT PUKED ON IT!
MEOW?!

HAHA, TOO BAD, HUH?
THANKS FOR THE GIFT. GOTTA RUN!
OH, HAPPY BIRTHDAY, SWEETIE!
THANKS, DAD!
HAVE FUN AT WORK!
ARE YOU ALL RIGHT, HIKARI?
SHE DIDN'T WEAR IT.

WELL, I TOLD YOU IT WAS GOING TO BE FUTILE.
YOU'RE SUPPOSED TO BE BACKING ME UP!
SHE'S SIXTEEN NOW! WHEN WILL SHE START ACTING LIKE A LADY?
C'MON, HIKARI. IT'S HER BIRTHDAY. CUT HER SOME SLA—
WE HAVE TO TELL HER TONIGHT, KAI!
IT'LL SNAP HER OUT OF THIS PHASE, AND SHE'LL BECOME THE WOMAN SHE'S DESTINED TO BE!
OH BOY.

North Luna High School
Huff
Huff
TAP
TAP
TAP
I GUESS I SHOULD INTRODUCE MYSELF. MY NAME IS MAX OWEN.
NORTH LUNA HIGH SCHOOL

NO RUNNING IN THE HALLS,
SORRY!

AT LEAST, THAT'S WHAT I WOULD LIKE TO BE CALLED.
IT'S SHORT AND SIMPLE AND AT THE SAME TIME, STRONG AND MANLY!

SQUEAK
TO GET TO THE POINT, I'M A TRANSGENDER MAN.

I HAVEN'T REALLY WORKED UP THE COURAGE TO COME OUT TO ANYBODY EXCEPT MY BEST FRIEND...
SQUEAK

YO, MAX!
JEN.

YOU SHOULD TOTALLY USE YOUR SPECIAL GIFT AND GUESS WHAT I'M FEELING!
AH!
AND TO THINK I COULDN'T BE WEIRDER, I GUESS I SHOULD ALSO MENTION...
I HAVE THIS WEIRD ABILITY TO SEE COLORED LIGHTS EMITTING OFF PEOPLE.
IT USUALLY REFLECTS HOW THEY'RE FEELING.

AT LEAST THAT'S MY ASSUMPTION. IT'S ALL FAIRLY NEW TO ME.
YOU KNOW...IT DOESN'T TAKE A GENIUS TO SEE YOU ARE OBVIOUSLY EXCITED ABOUT SOMETHING.
HAHA, YOU'RE RIGHT.
WHAT WOULD PEOPLE EVEN CALL THIS?
AURA?
CHI?
LIGHT ENERGY?

LIGHT FARTS?
I HAVE NO IDEA.

HAPPY BIRTHDAY, MAX!
AH, THANK YOU!
RING
RING
RING

JEN IS THE BEST—I REALLY DON'T KNOW WHERE I'D BE WITHOUT HER.
I MEAN, ON TOP OF TRYING TO TRANSITION...
I HAVE THIS TO DEAL WITH.
I JUST WANT TO BE A NORMAL BOY. IS THAT TOO MUCH TO ASK?

SLAM
MAX, DID YOU OPEN THE GIFT YET?

AH, NOT YET.
DUDE, WHAT ARE YOU WAITING FOR? OPEN IT NOW!

OKAY, OKAY.
CRINKLE

GASP!
NO WAY! IS THIS WHAT I THINK IT IS?!
YUP, IT'S ONE OF THOSE CHEST COMPRESSORS.
NOW YOU DON'T HAVE TO KEEP USING THESE TIGHT MIDDLE SCHOOL SPORTS BRAS TO HIDE YOUR CHEST.
I'M TRYING THIS ON NOW!

LET ME KNOW IF YOU NEED HELP.
NAH, I GOT THIS.
WAIT, NO, I THINK I'M STUCK.

HAHA, SERIOUSLY, MAX? LET ME HELP YOU.
EXIT
UGH, WHY DO YOU KEEP CALLING HER MAX?

NEWS FLASH, SHE'S NOT A BOY AND HER NAME IS .
NO, IT'S MAX AND I'M A BOY!
BUT I CAN'T SAY THAT OUT LOUD.
MIND YOUR OWN BUSINESS, PYPER.

RUDE AS EVER...
AND TO THINK WE USED TO BE FRIENDS WHEN WE WERE LITTLE.
PYPER IS THE DAUGHTER OF A PASTOR OF A NEARBY PROMINENT CHRISTIAN CHURCH.
SHE'S SCARY AND THE LAST PERSON I WOULD EVER WANT TO COME OUT TO.
GOOD RIDDANCE. I WOULDN'T WANT TO BE FRIENDS WITH SOME LESBIAN ANYWAY.
OH MAN, I'M SO SORRY, JEN!
HER LIGHT FART IS EVEN DARKER THAN YESTERDAY.

WHAT IS YOUR PROB-
RUMBLE
RUMBLE
RUMBLE
AN EARTHQUAKE?!
RUMBLE
WHY IS THERE AN-
AHHH!
SLIP
RUMBLE
RUMBLE

SSSSSS
THUMP
!
YOU OKAY?
LOOK AT CHU—GETTING ALL BOLD ALL OF A SUDDEN.

YOU W-WISH.
BWAHH BWAHH BAHH
ATTENTION PLEASE, THIS IS NOT A DRILL. PLEASE EXIT THE BUILDING IMMEDIATELY.
EXIT
BWAH BWAHHH
YOU ALL RIGHT, MAX?

YEAH, I EVEN MANAGED TO GET THE BINDER ON.
BWAHH BWAHH
BWAHH BWAHH
NICE! LOOKIN' FLAT AS A BOARD.
NOW YOU JUST NEED A HAIRCUT!
GASP
YES!

EXIT

THERE'S SOMETHING ON YOU!

AHH, WHERE?!
...
NOTHING
UGH! YOU DEGENERATES! HOW CAN YOU TWO PLAY JOKES AFTER SOMETHING LIKE THIS?!
TCK
TCK
MELODRAMATIC MUCH? THE EARTHQUAKE WASN'T EVEN THAT BAD.
EXIT
SLAM

ANYWAYS, GOOD ONE, MAX.
I REALLY THOUGHT I SAW SOMETHING. I GUESS NOT...
C'MON, LET'S GET OUT OF HERE AND SEE WHAT'S GOING ON.
HM.
DO YOU THINK ANY PARTS OF THE SCHOOL WERE DAMAGED?
I'M JUST HOPING THERE ISN'T ANOTHER ONE.
TCK
TCK
WIGGLE
WIGGLE

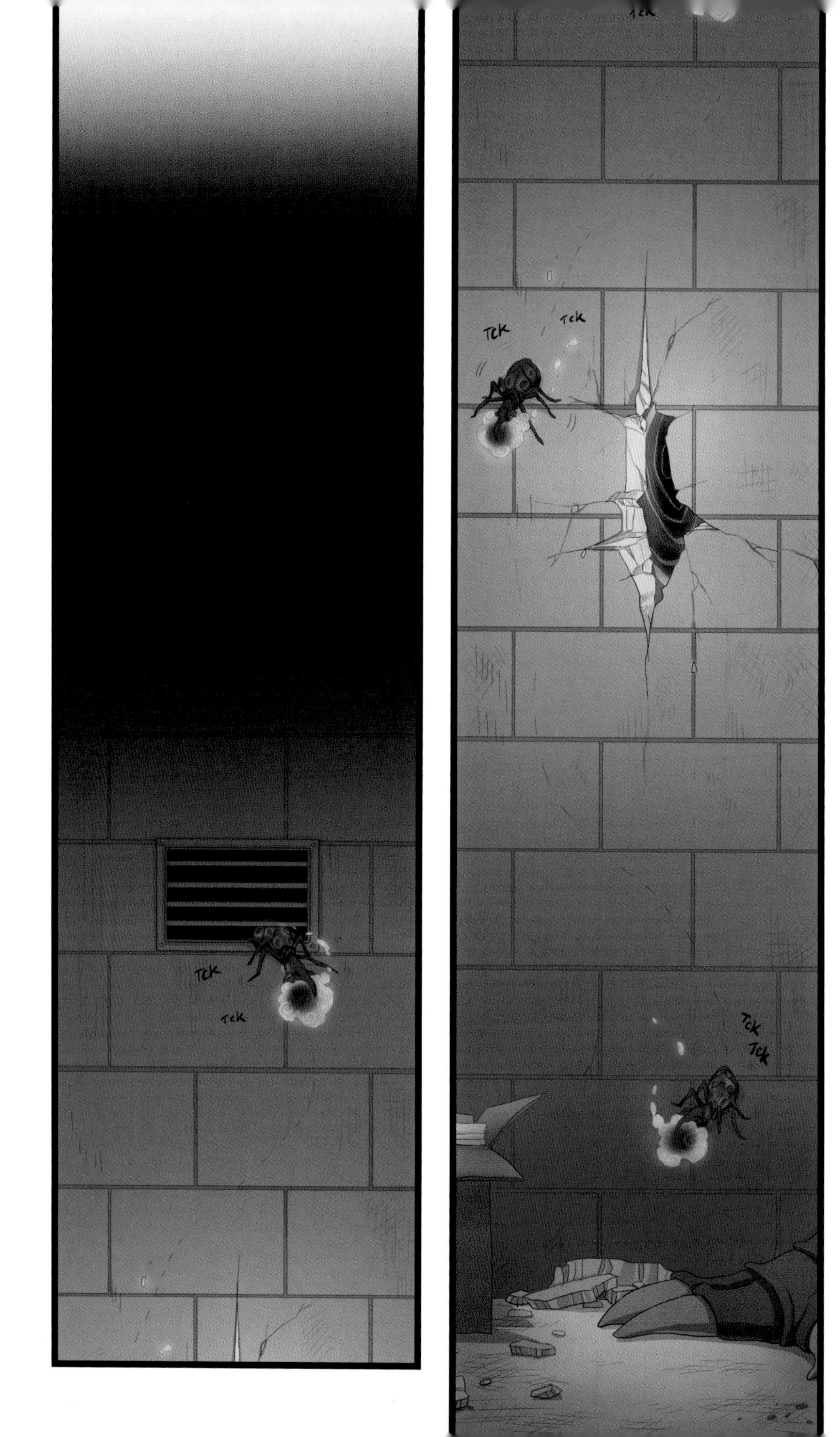

TCK
TCK
TCK
TCK
TCK
TCK

KEKEKE, THE TIME HAS COME—

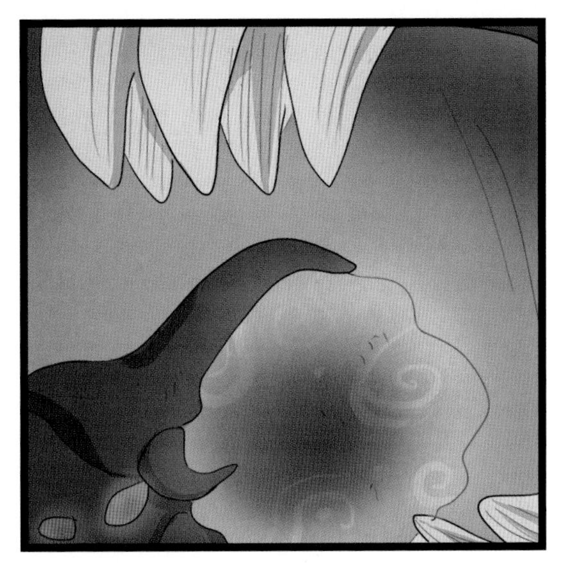

CHOMP!
I WILL NOT DISAPPOINT YOU, MY KING.

Episode 2:
COMING OUT

A 3.3 MAGNITUDE EARTHQUAKE OCCURRED EARLIER THIS AFTERNOON IN DOWNTOWN CHICAGO.
ALTHOUGH RARE, MINOR EARTHQUAKES DO OCCUR IN THIS AREA ABOUT ONCE EVERY YEAR.
WHERE ON EARTH IS ?
IT'S BEEN HOURS SINCE SCHOOL'S BEEN OUT. YOU'D THINK SHE WOULD CALL AFTER AN EARTHQUAKE.
NO SERIOUS DAMAGES OR INJURIES WERE REPORTED IN THE CHICAGO AREA.
BIRTHDAY
SHE'S PROBABLY HANGING OUT WITH HER FRIENDS.
IT **IS** HER BIRTHDAY. AND LIKE THE NEWS SAID, THE EARTHQUAKE WASN'T BAD.

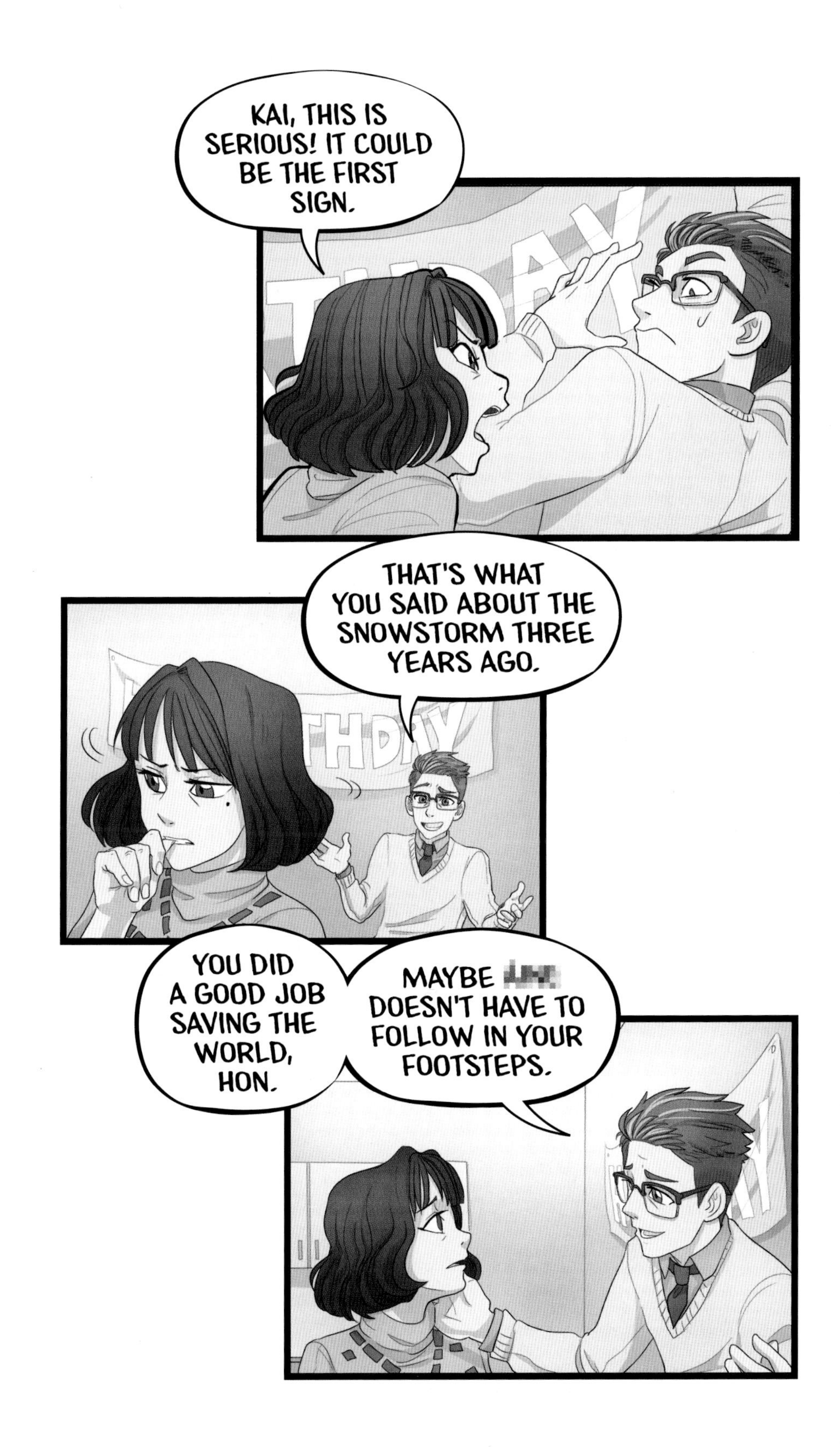
KAI, THIS IS SERIOUS! IT COULD BE THE FIRST SIGN.
THAT'S WHAT YOU SAID ABOUT THE SNOWSTORM THREE YEARS AGO.
YOU DID A GOOD JOB SAVING THE WORLD, HON.
MAYBE DOESN'T HAVE TO FOLLOW IN YOUR FOOTSTEPS.

MAYBE...
JINGLE
CREAK
SLAM
step
step

WELCOME HOME, SWEETIE. WE GOT YOUR FAVORITE CAKE.

WE NEED TO TALK.

OH NO...
DID I GET THE WRONG CAKE?
HAPPY BIRTHDA
NO, IT'S PERFECT.
IT'S SOMETHING ELSE, AND I THINK YOU TWO SHOULD SIT DOWN FOR THIS.

HAPP
...
INHALE

IT'S ABOUT TIME I COME CLEAN WITH YOU GUYS.
YOU'RE DOING DRUGS?

WHAT? NO.
I MEAN, I'M TRYING TO BE STRAIGHT-FORWARD AND COME OUT...
SO YOU'RE GAY.
YOU LIKE GIRLS?
YES.
WAIT, NO. DAD!

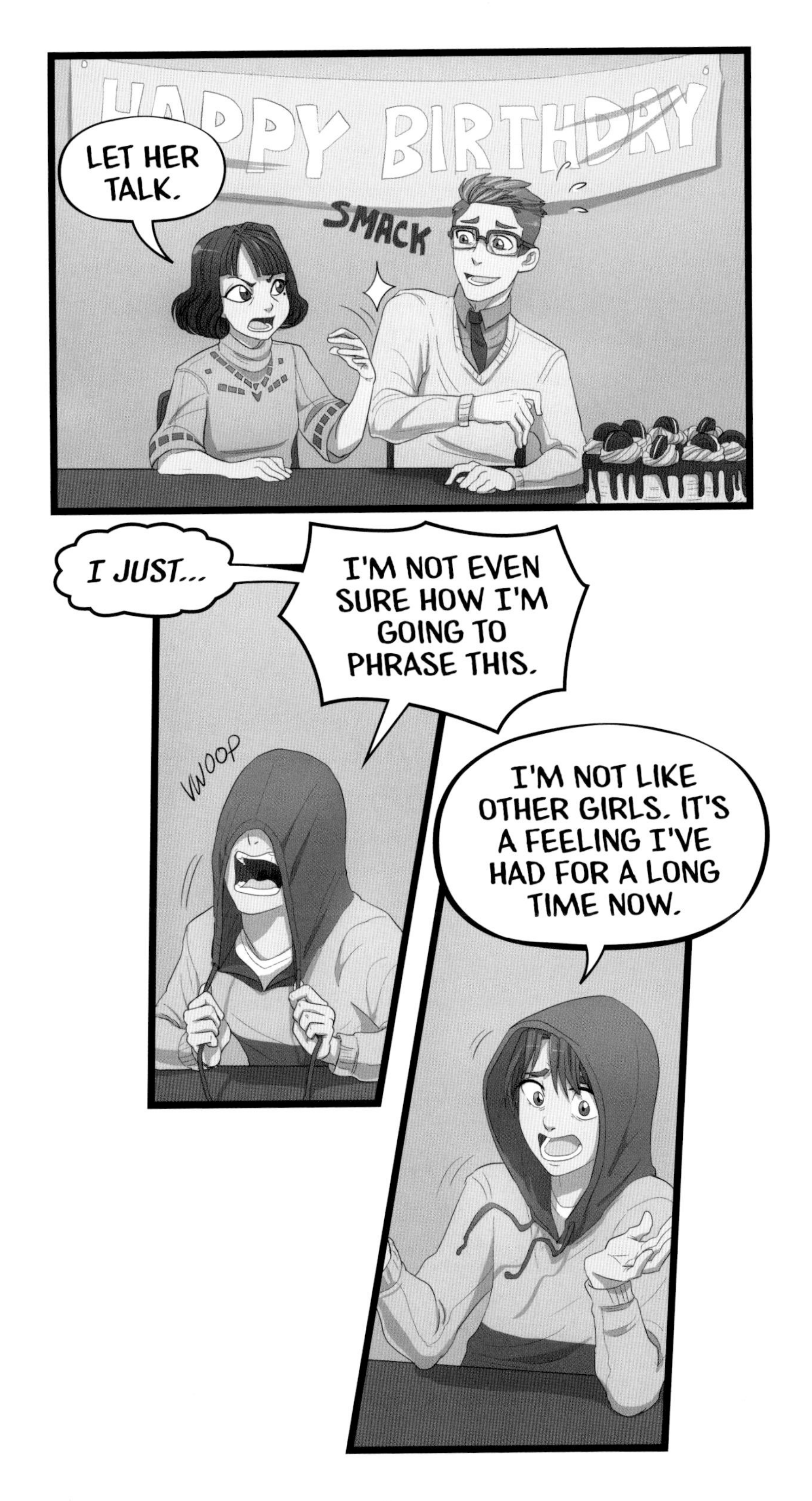
HAPPY BIRTHDAY
LET HER TALK.
SMACK
I JUST...
I'M NOT EVEN SURE HOW I'M GOING TO PHRASE THIS.
VWOOP
I'M NOT LIKE OTHER GIRLS. IT'S A FEELING I'VE HAD FOR A LONG TIME NOW.

!
?
PAT PAT
I KNOW YOU WANT ME TO BE THIS PERFECT LITTLE GIRL. I'VE BEEN STRUGGLING TO ACCEPT IT ALL MY LIFE.
ESPECIALLY WHEN I HIT PUBERTY.
GASP!
IT?

BEING A GIRL!
MY APPEARANCE.
MY BODY.
NONE OF IT MATCHES THE PERSON I AM DEEP INSIDE...
WHO'S DESPERATELY TRYING TO COME OUT.

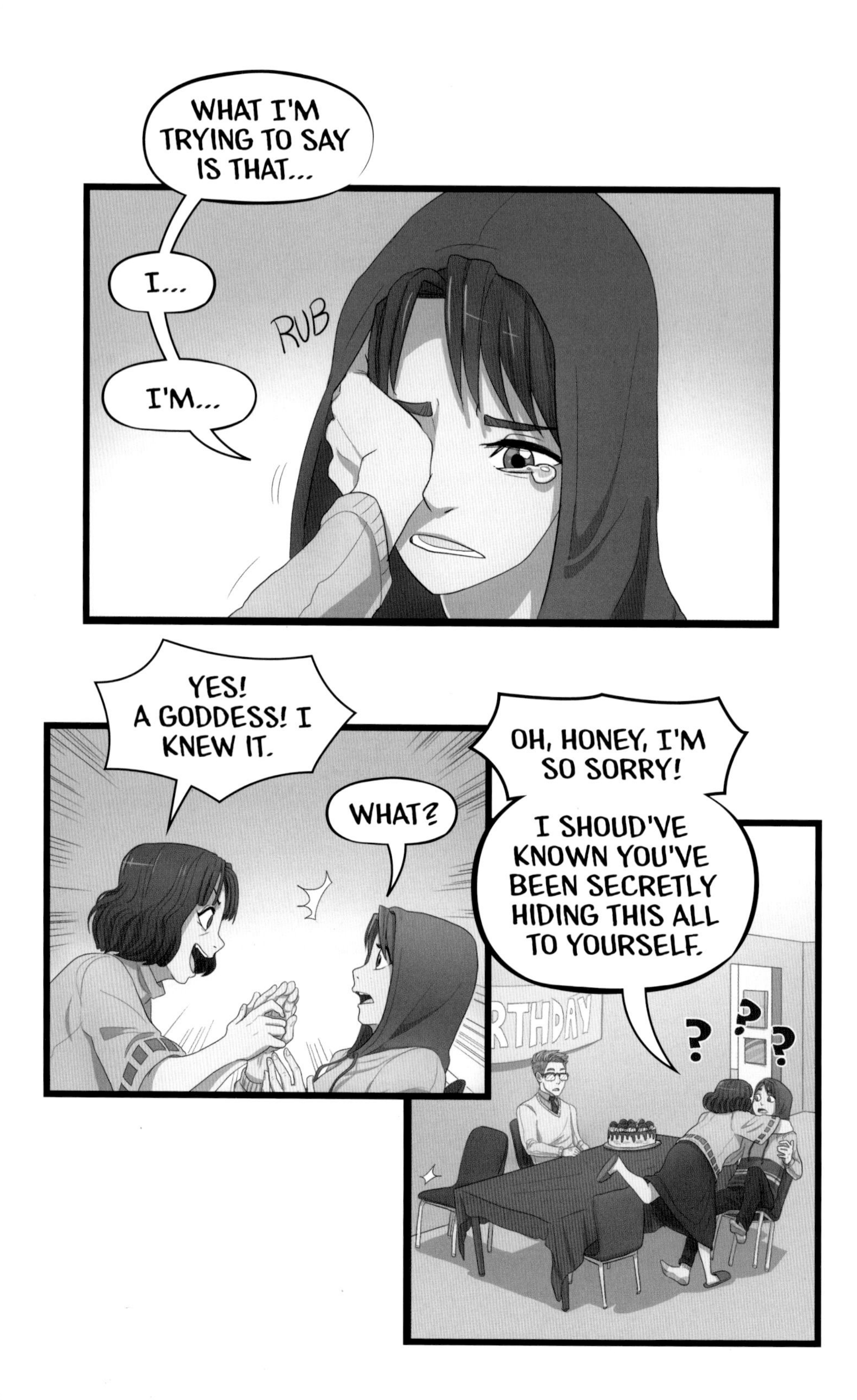
WHAT I'M TRYING TO SAY IS THAT...
I...
I'M...
RUB
YES! A GODDESS! I KNEW IT.
WHAT?
OH, HONEY, I'M SO SORRY!
I SHOUD'VE KNOWN YOU'VE BEEN SECRETLY HIDING THIS ALL TO YOURSELF.
RTHDAY
?
?
?

I KNEW I SHOULD'VE TOLD YOU SOONER. ANY SANE PERSON WOULD BE CONFUSED AND THINK THEY ARE INSANE THE FIRST TIME.
WHAT ARE YOU TALKING ABOUT?
, IT'S OKAY. YOU DON'T HAVE TO HIDE ANYMORE.
THESE FEELINGS ARE NORMAL IN OUR BLOODLINE.
NORMAL? REALLY?

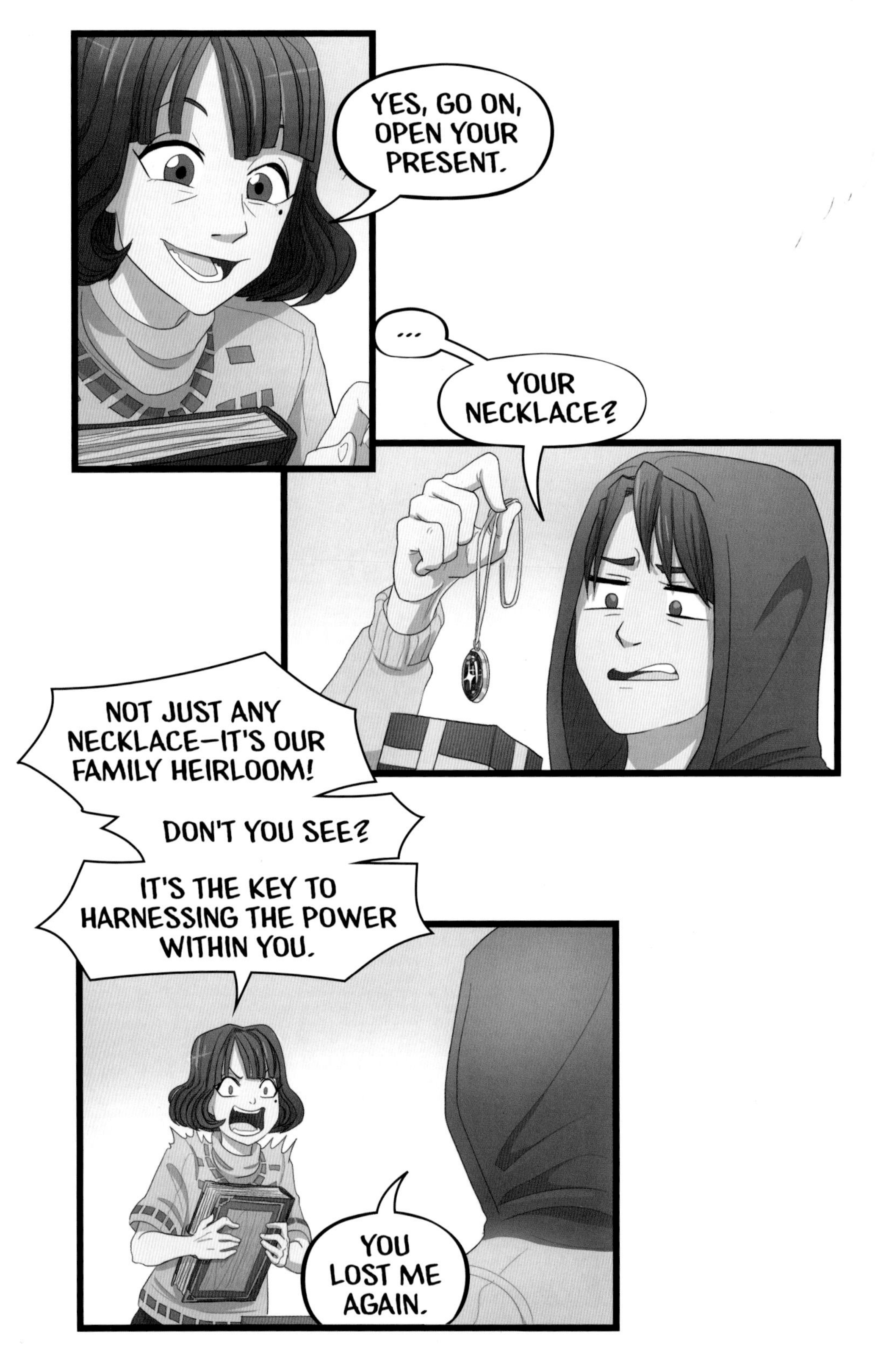
YES, GO ON, OPEN YOUR PRESENT.
...
YOUR NECKLACE?
NOT JUST ANY NECKLACE—IT'S OUR FAMILY HEIRLOOM!
DON'T YOU SEE?
IT'S THE KEY TO HARNESSING THE POWER WITHIN YOU.
YOU LOST ME AGAIN.

LOOK, REMEMBER THIS? I USED TO READ THIS TO YOU WHEN YOU WERE A BABY.
THE STORIES ARE ALL TRUE, HONEY.
WE ARE THE DESCENDANTS OF AURORA, THE GODDESS OF LIGHT!

IT'S NOW TIME TO FULFILL YOUR DESTINY AS THE NEXT GODDESS IN LINE!
WAIT, YOU MEAN THAT CLICHÉ STORY WHERE LIGHT HAS TO FIGHT THE MONSTERS?
YES!
WAIT, NO! IT'S NOT CLICHÉ, AND I AM BEING SERIOUS.

SO OF COURSE YOU'RE NOT LIKE OTHER GIRLS.
YOU ARE MORE THAN THAT...
AND YOUR INNER POWERS ARE JUST TRYING TO CALL OUT TO YOU.
IT IS NOW YOUR DUTY TO CHASE THE COMING DARKNESS AWAY. I WAS WORRIED FOR A SECOND THERE!
YOU STILL HAVEN'T SHOWN ANY SIGNS, BUT YOU WERE HOLDING BACK ON THESE FEELINGS.
MOM...
THIS IS CRAZY. WHAT I'M TRYING TO SAY IS—
I AM SO HAPPY FOR YOU. BUT WE SHOULDN'T WAIT—YOU NEED TO CATCH UP AND PREPARE.
MOM, LISTEN!

WHAT DID YOU DO TO YOUR HAIR!
I'M A MAN.
ARE YOU OUT OF YOUR MIND? DID YOU NOT HEAR ME?
YOU HAVE THE BLOOD OF A GODDESS.
YOU MEAN FROM THIS STUPID CHILDREN'S BOOK YOU NEVER LET ME READ BY MYSELF?
IT'S JUST A STUPID FAIRY TALE!
FWP

DON'T SAY THAT!
I HAVEN'T BEEN TRYING TO MAKE YOU A PROPER LADY FOR NOTHING!
THAT'S WHAT I'M TRYING TO TELL YOU. I'M NOT A LADY.
I'VE ALWAYS FELT LIKE A MAN!
THAT'S CLEARLY NONSENSE! THE GODDESS IS A WOMAN. YOU ARE A WOMAN.
IT'S TIME YOU START ACTING LIKE ONE.

I KNEW YOU WOULDN'T LISTEN.
YOU CAN TAKE YOUR "FAMILY HEIRLOOM" BACK. I DON'T WANT ANY OF THIS!
THUNK

WHERE ARE YOU GOING? YOU CAN'T RUN AWAY FROM THIS!

YOU TOO?!
PIT PAT

SIGH
WHAT ARE WE GONG TO DO WITH HER, KAI?

KAI?
HAPPY BIRTHDAY

WOO, OUR BABY IS A BOY?
HAPPY BIRTHDAY
POP

NO! SHE'S JUST CONFUSED.
HONESTLY, KAI, WHY AREN'T YOU BACKING ME UP?
YOU KNOW WHAT'S AT STAKE.
UHH

HEY...
WHERE DID
THE HEIRLOOM
GO?

I
THINK THE
CAT TOOK
IT.

TIK
TIK
JEN
How'd it go?
Absolutely terrible, can we meet up?

That bad, huh? The usual place?
Yeah, I can use some shaved ice and bubble tea right now.

RUSTLE

RUSTLE
RUSTLE
CLACK
CLACK
CLACK
CLACK
CLACK

WALNUT?
CLACK

HOLY SHA-

UMP
FWIN
HISSSSSSS
FWUP

DON'T TELL ME THIS IS PART OF MOM'S...

...CRAZY STORY ABOUT MONSTERS.
!
HEY, WAIT! YOU GET BACK HERE!
SKIT
SKIT SKIT
SKIT SKIT
SKIT SKIT

DAMN IT.

BUBBLE TEA HOUSE

BUBBLE

Episode 3:
IMPOSSIBLE

TIK
TIK
TIK
TIK
TIK
TIK
TIK
TIK
TIK
TIK
TIK
TIK
TIK
TIK
TIK

TAP
TAP
TAP

I GOT YOU NOW!
!
WHOOP
EH?!

THUMP
SKIT
SKIT
SKIT
SKIT

EXIT
THUD
EXIT
WHERE DID YOU GO?
YOU LITTLE...
POKE

AH!
WHOA, WHOA! IT'S ME, MAX!
OH, SORRY, I THOUGHT YOU WERE A BUG.
WOW, YOUR PARENTS MUST HAVE REALLY MESSED YOU UP...

SO LET ME GET THIS STRAIGHT.
YOUR MOM IS AGAINST YOU BEING TRANS BECAUSE YOU COME FROM A BLOODLINE OF SOME FEMININE DEITY THAT NEEDS TO FIGHT MONSTERS?
I DUNNO. THAT SOUNDS KINDA COOL.
WHAT?!
SHE'S INSANE, JEN.
IT WAS FROM THIS STUPID BOOK SHE ALWAYS READ TO ME AS A KID.

EVEN SO, I HAVE TO SAY, IT KINDA MAKES SENSE WHY YOU CAN SEE LIGHT AROUND PEOPLE.
IT'S YOUR SUPERPOWER.
YOU'RE HALFWAY TO BECOMING MAGICAL GIRL.
NO WAY! I WOULDN'T BE CAUGHT DEAD WEARING SOME RIDICULOUS FRILLY COSTUME! AND SEEING LIGHT DOESN'T DO JACK. I CAN'T FIGHT WITH THAT.
EVEN IF THIS IS SOME KIND OF DESTINY CRAP, IT SHOULDN'T MATTER WHAT GENDER I AM. I CAN STILL FIGHT EITHER WAY.

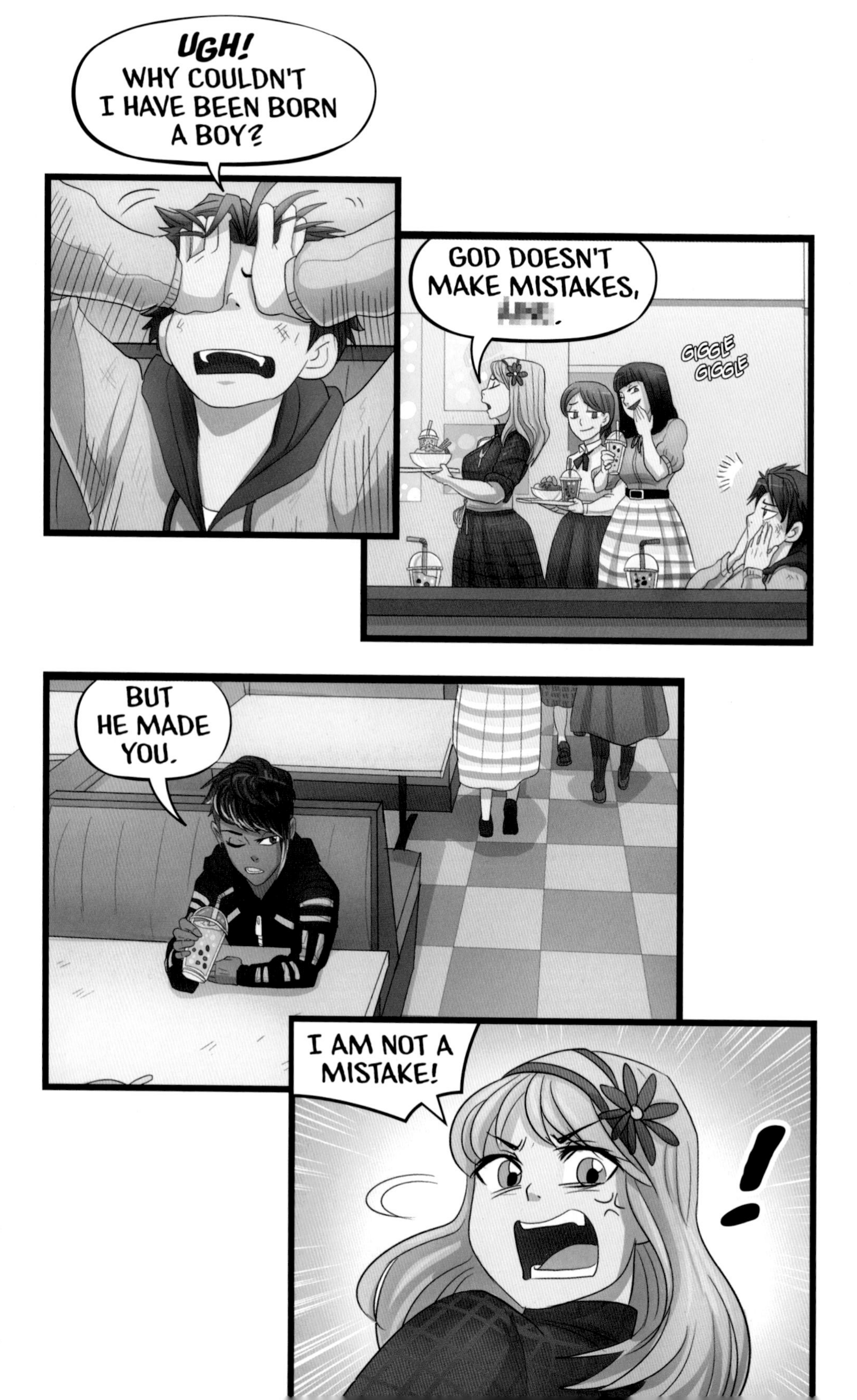
UGH! WHY COULDN'T I HAVE BEEN BORN A BOY?
GOD DOESN'T MAKE MISTAKES,
GIGGLE GIGGLE
BUT HE MADE YOU.
I AM NOT A MISTAKE!
!

UNLIKE YOU TWO, WHO ARE CLEARLY THE DEVIL'S WORK, OPENLY COMMITTING YOUR SINS.
YEAH, YOU SHOULD BE ASHAMED OF YOURSELVES.
NO ONE WANTS TO SEE YOUR GAY ROMANCE.
I DIDN'T KNOW COMING HERE WITH A FRIEND FOR DRINKS AND ICE CREAM WAS GAY.
DOES THAT MEAN YOU'RE HERE FOR A THREESOME WITH PYPER?
HOW DARE YOU!
STOP TRYING TO MAKE EVERYONE GAY LIKE YOU!
EVERYONE KNOWS YOU TWO ARE DATING!
THIS ISN'T GOOD...

HAHAHA! YES! KEEP FIGHTING!
YOU!
HISSSSS!
AH, SPIDER!

AHHHHHHHHHHH
TIC
TAK
TIC

AHHHHHHHHH
MAX. WAIT UP!
HHA

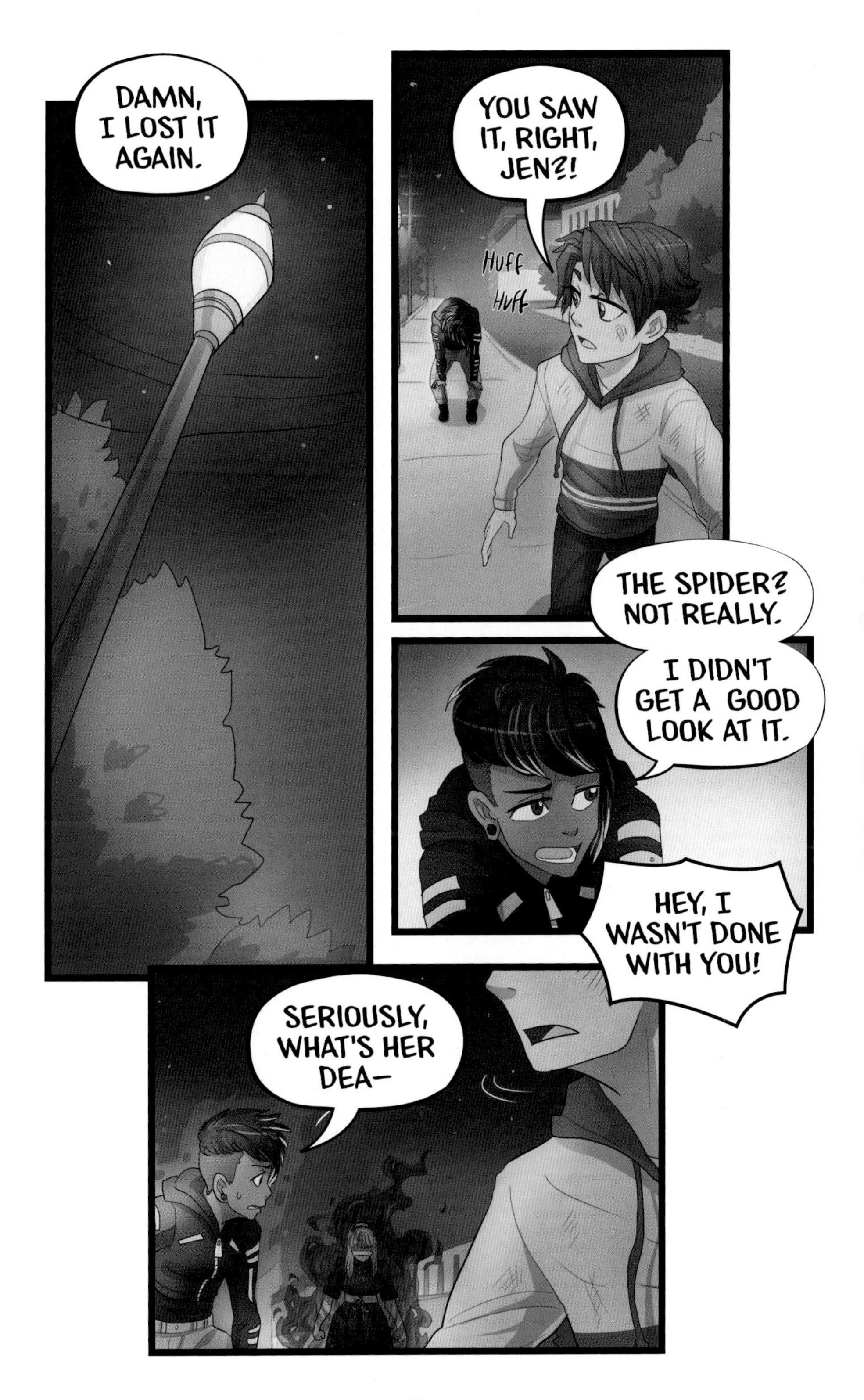
DAMN, I LOST IT AGAIN.
YOU SAW IT, RIGHT, JEN?!
HUFF
HUFF
THE SPIDER? NOT REALLY.
I DIDN'T GET A GOOD LOOK AT IT.
HEY, I WASN'T DONE WITH YOU!
SERIOUSLY, WHAT'S HER DEA—

I AM NOT A MISTAKE. THERE'S NOTHING WRONG WITH ME.
IS IT ME, OR IS THERE A GIANT BUG-LIKE THING ON HER BACK?
IT GOT BIGGER...
I'M FOLLOWING THE BIBLE LIKE A GOOD GIRL. KEEPING THE DEVIL AT BAY.
BUT WHY DO I HAVE TO SUFFER?
WHY DO THEY GET TO BE HAPPY?

IT'S NOT FAIR!

THUD

HAHAHA! PATHETIC HUMAN. SO FULL OF SELF-HATRED AND SADNESS.
AT THIS RATE, I'LL FLY THROUGH THE RANKS AND BE UNSTOPPABLE!
WHAM

THAT'S FOR MESSIN' WITH ME EARLIER!
THUNK
NICE ONE, MAX!
HOW'S PYPER?
SHE'S STILL BREATHING BUT IT'S FAINT.
WHAT DID THAT THING DO TO HER?
I'M NOT SURE, BUT IT LOOKED LIKE IT WAS EATING HER LIGHT.
WHAT? FOR REAL?

YOU WILL PAY FOR THAT!

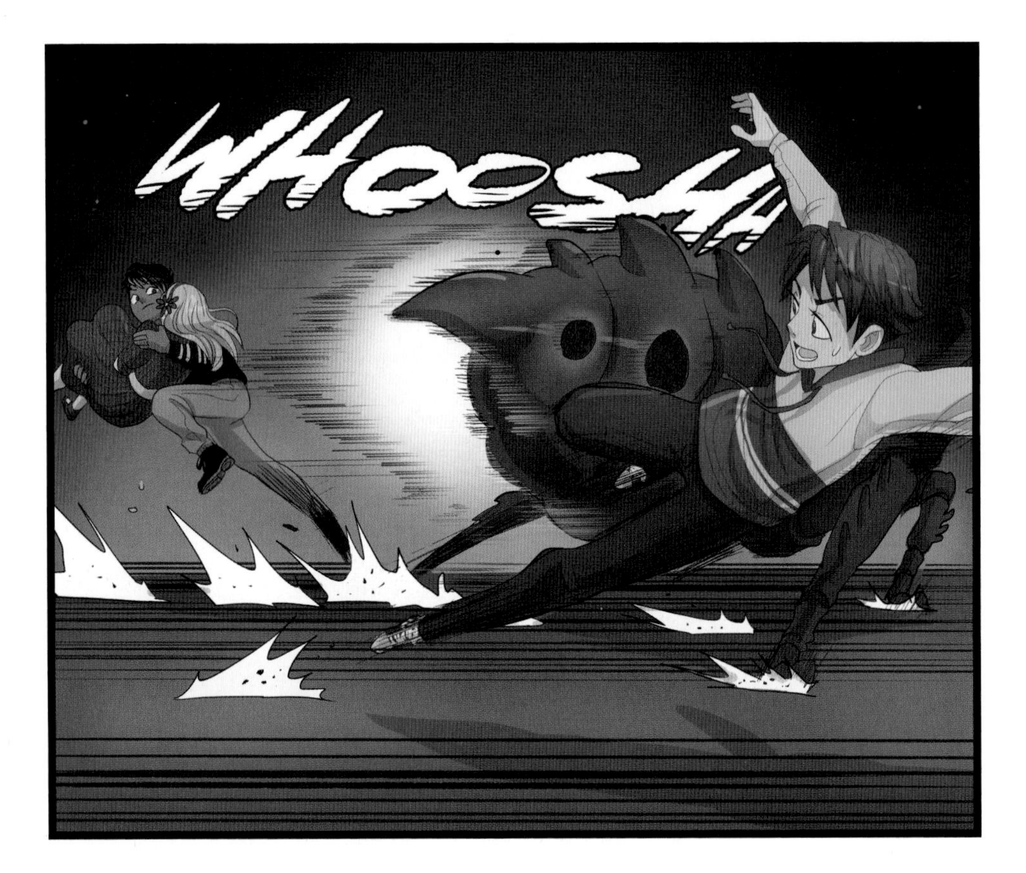
WHOOSH

SHHHHHHH

FWOOP
ptt
ptt
ptt
WHOA!
ACK!

UGH, GROSS.
STOMP
STOMP
STOMP
OH NO, YOU DON'T!
WHAM

YEAH, MAX, BEAT THAT THING TO A PULP!
WHACK
WHACK
WHACK
WHACK
YOU'RE SO LUCKY WE'RE SAVING YOUR ASS.
I DON'T THINK THIS IS WORKING. ITS SKIN IS TOO TOUGH.
...I GUESS WE SHOULD HAVE RUN, HUH?

I'LL DESTROY YOU!
WHACK
DON'T YOU GO DYING NOW!
I GOT THIS.

!

MAX!
PA-TOU

YOU LITTLE–
MEOW!
SLASH
!!
WALNUT?!
THUNK

...
DON'T TELL ME YOU'RE SECRETLY MY ANIMAL SIDEKICK.
HUFF
BLEH
HUFF
I'M MORE LIKE YOUR GUARDIAN.
SON OF A—

YOU WILL PAY!
YOU NEED TO USE THE AMULET NOW!
STOMP
STOMP
STOMP
NO!
STOMP
WHAT DO YOU MEAN, NO?!
I AM NOT TURNING INTO SOME MAGICAL GIRL!
MAGICAL GIRL? PLEASE. YOU WILL BE TRANSFORMING INTO A GODDESS!

!
THAT'S NOT ANY BETTER!
AND I'LL BE CLIPPING YOUR CLAWS AFTER THIS!
SLASH

BLAMM

DIE!
!

BING
W-WHAT IS THIS?!

IN THE BEGINNING

Long,
long, ago...
there lived a goddess,
Aurora.
She embodied
the power
of light.

It was she who
shined light on
the planet

against the dark deity.

He who plagued the
lands with darkness for
many centuries...

with Aurora's light

of hope, love,
and compassion,

all living
creatures

!

were able to
flourish with
overwhelming
life force.

that gave Devoid strength.

Tired of living in the shadows,

he began a reign of terror among the people with his monstrous creatures...

creating increasing amounts of fear, anger, and greed among them.

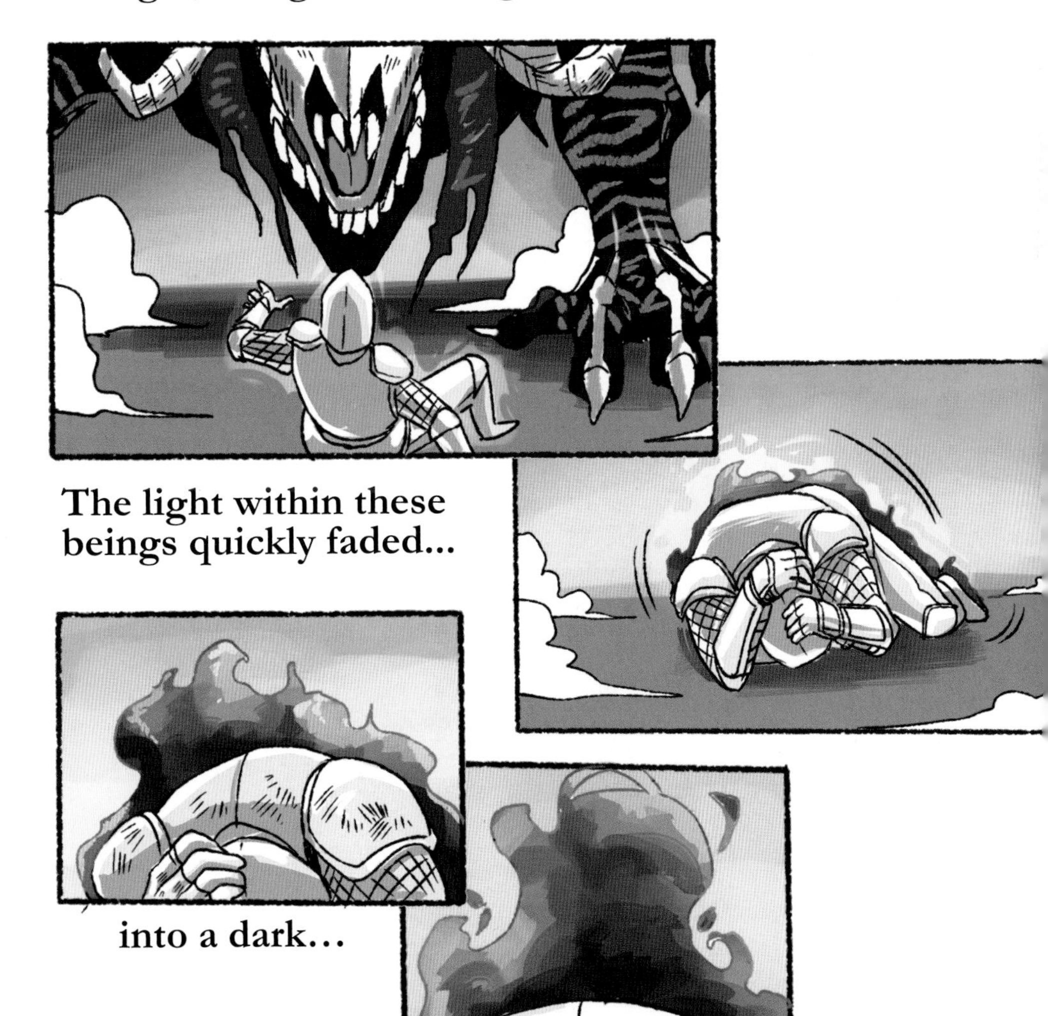

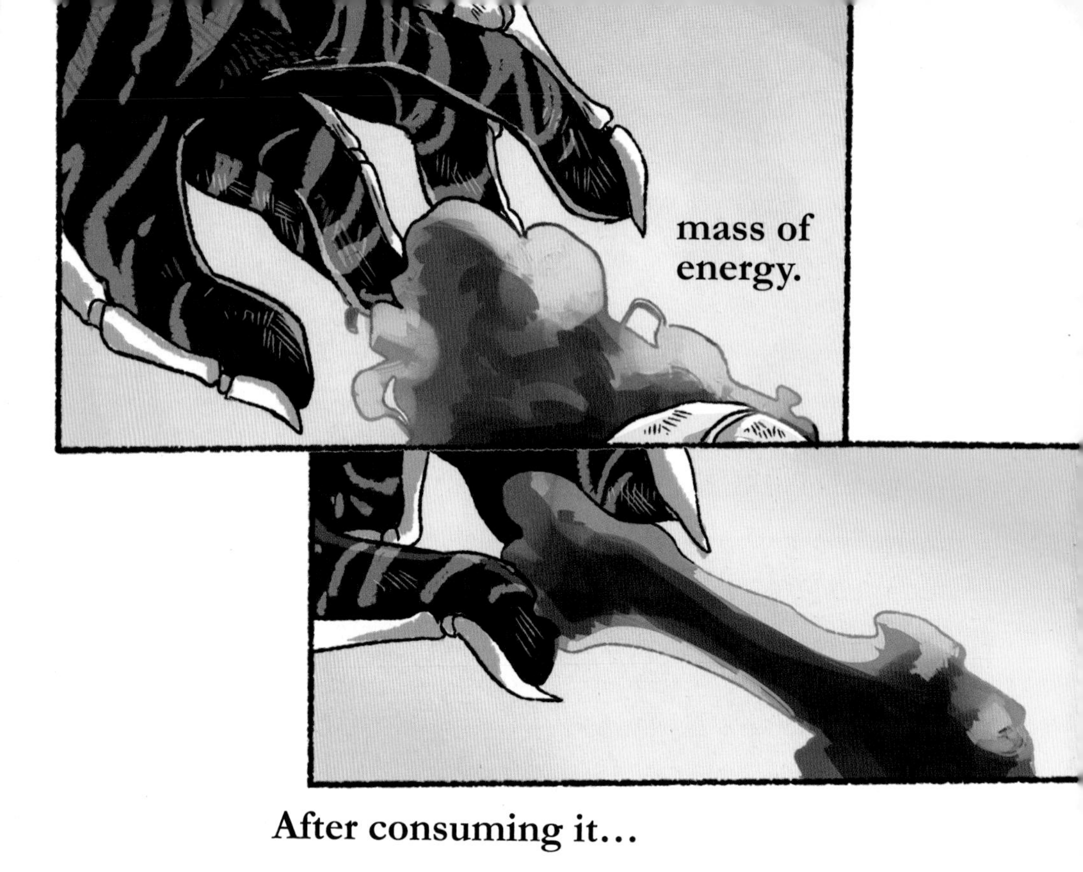
mass of energy.
After consuming it…

Devoid became…

unstoppable!

Aurora knew she had to do something

before it was too late.

With the help of her trusty guardian,

they dove into battle

with bursting

light!

They imprisoned Devoid
in another realm…

in hopes that
he would
never return.

But in doing so...

Aurora sacrificed
her very being . . .

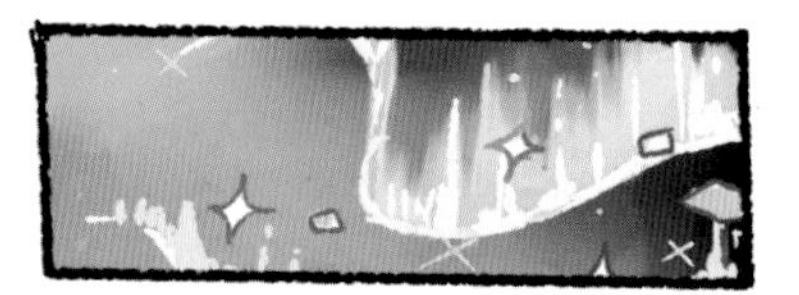

to withhold
the seal...

AND NOW IT'S UP TO US...

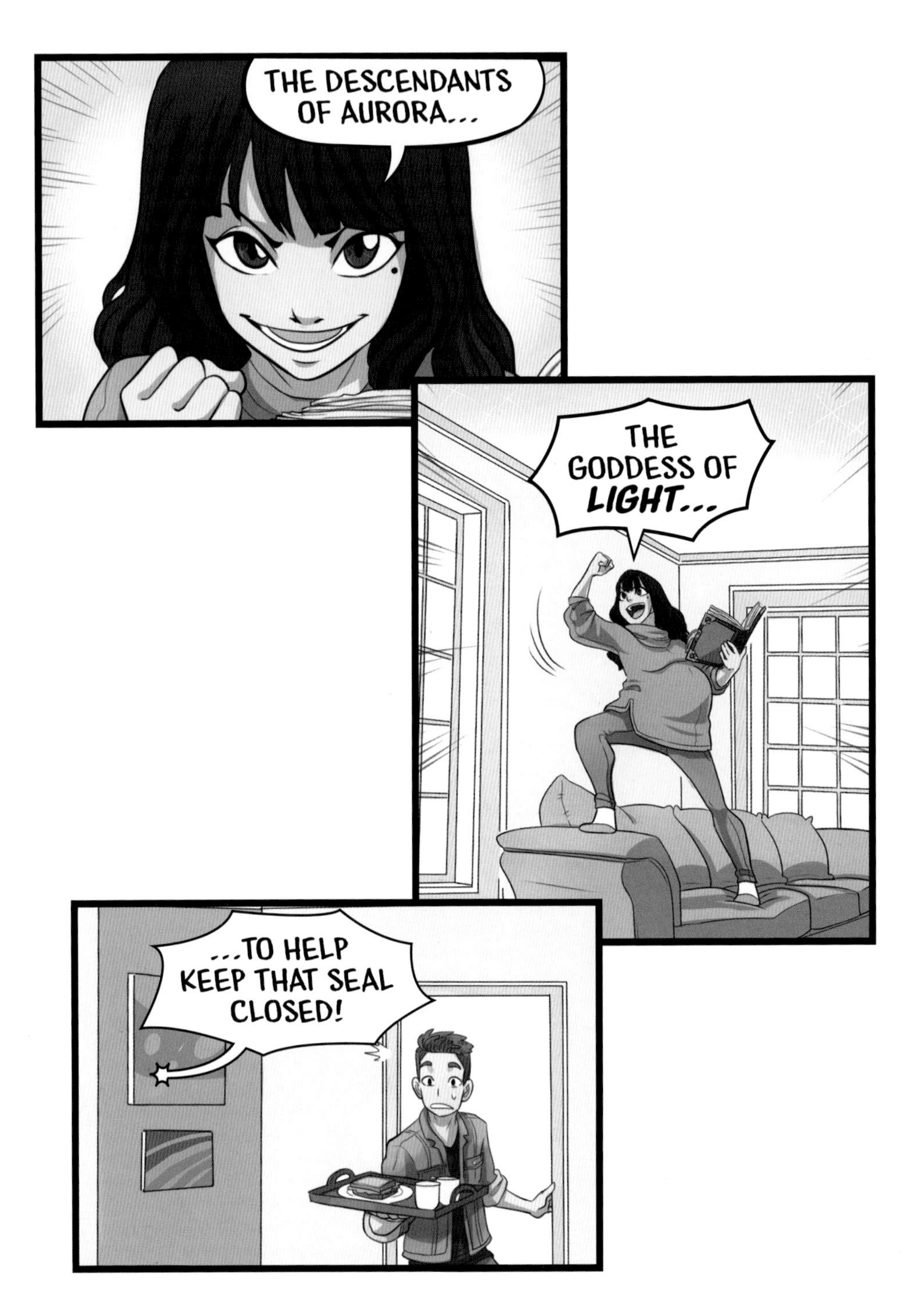
THE DESCENDANTS OF AURORA...
THE GODDESS OF LIGHT...
...TO HELP KEEP THAT SEAL CLOSED!

HIKARI, YOU SHOULDN'T GET TOO RILED UP.
YOU'LL PUT TOO MUCH STRAIN ON THE BABY.

IT'S FINE. SHE IS STRONG LIKE ME.

DON'T YOU AGREE?
mew

OH! AND I CAME UP WITH A NAME—
OH?
! AFTER THE GODDESS OF LOVE, GROWTH, AND LIGHT. HER VERY NAME MEANS "TO LIGHT AGAINST THE DARKNESS"!
...
AT LEAST ACCORDING TO SOURCES ONLINE...

OWEN?
DIDN'T YOU SAY YOU LIKED MY LAST NAME BECAUSE IT REFERENCED SOME OTHER GODDESS OF LIGHT?
YOU DIDN'T JUST MARRY ME FOR THE NAME, DID YOU?
WHAT? DON'T BE SILLY...
COUGH

WHAT WAS THAT?
NOTHING, I'M JUST KIDDING—
ANYWAYS... WITH ALL JOKES ASIDE,
WHAT IF...
OUR BABY...

...IS A BOY?
SMACK
DON'T BE RIDICULOUS!
YOU KNOW FROM THE BOOK THAT MY FAMILY COMES FROM A LONG LINE OF ONLY WOMEN!
THE FATE OF THE WORLD DEPENDS ON IT!
SORRY I ASKED...

Episode 4:

MOMENT OF TRUTH

BACK IN THE PRESENT...

AM I
DEAD?

IT'S TIME
TO SHINE.
HUH? WHO
SAID THAT?

WHOOOSH

WHOA!

WHAT'S HAPPENING TO MY CLOTHES?!

AH! NOT MY BINDER!

NOOOO!
I JUST GOT THIS!

AAAAHH
AAAAAH!

WAIT! NOT THE HAIR, TOO!
PING

WHOOOOOSHH
REALLY?

WHOOSH
SHHHHH
WHOOSH
TING

PING
BING

THIS IS SO UNNECESSARY!

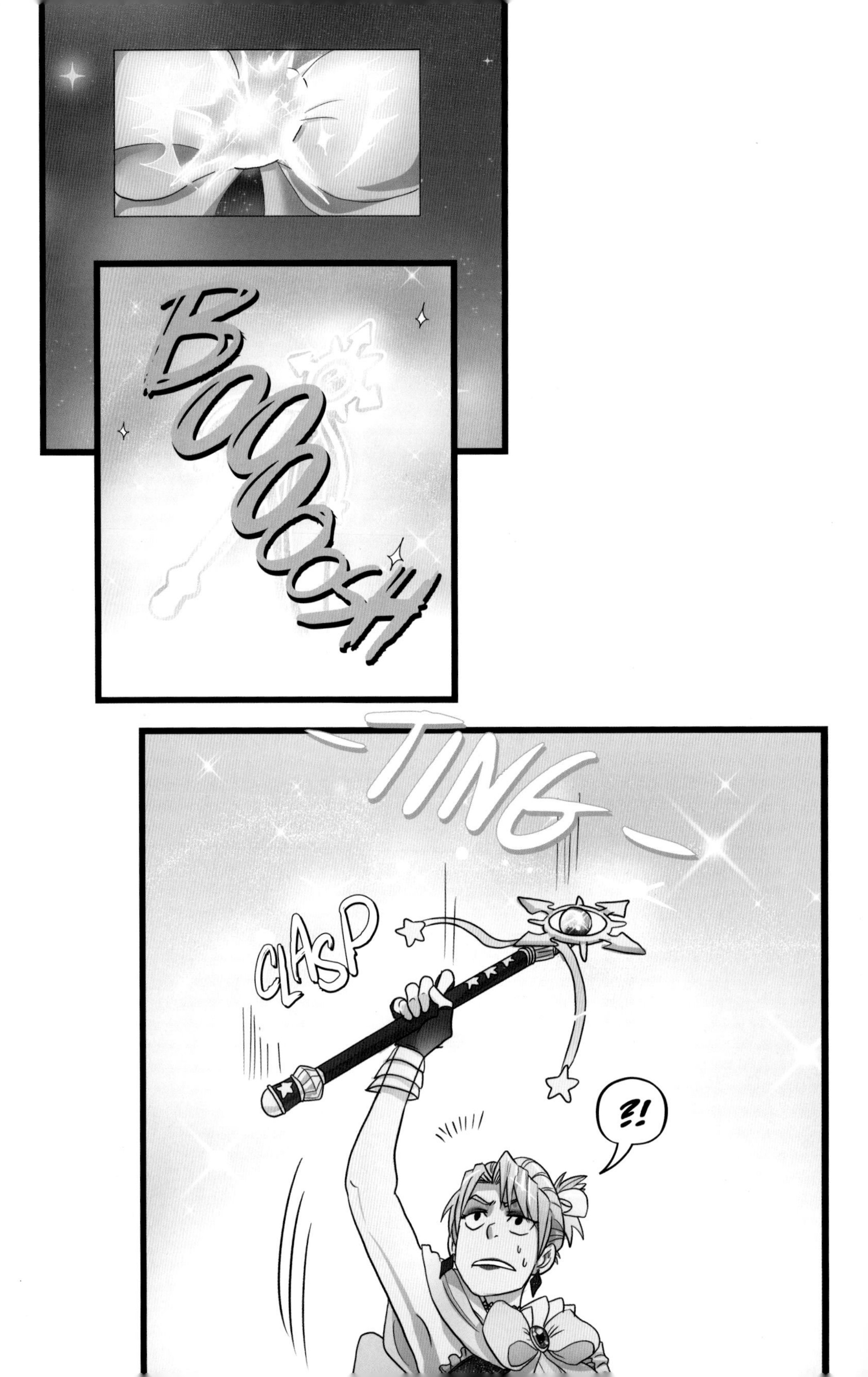
BOOOOOSH
TING
CLASP
?!

DAMN IT!
MY EYES!
I FEEL SO VIOLATED.
QUICKLY NOW, USE THE POWER OF THE GODDESS TO VANQUISH THE DARKNESS!
OH SNAP.

AHHH!

!
OH, COME ON!
HEELS ARE SO IMPRACTICAL!
YANK
THUNK
?!
HOW DARE Y—

WH ACK
NO! WHAT ARE YOU DOING?!
I'M USING THE HEIRLOOM TO ATTACK IT—ISN'T THAT WHAT I'M SUPPOSED TO DO?
YOU DON'T SWING IT AROUND LIKE A BARBARIAN!
WHAM
WHERE IS YOUR BALANCE? WHERE IS YOUR GRACE?!

WHAT?!
MEOW MEOW!
THAT DOESN'T MAKE SENSE.
MEOW!
• • •
STOP TELLING ME WHAT TO DO!
JUST WIGGLE IT A LITTLE!

FINE!
WHOOSH
WHOOSH
...
BOOM!!
HAHAHA! HOW PATHE—
AAAHH!

AAAHHHHHH!!
SHHHHH!!
HHHH
SHHHHH
HHHHH
YES! FINALLY, I'M FREE!
UGH.
!
WHOOPS, I GOTCHU.
COUGH, COUGH.

SEE, WHAT DID I TELL YOU? I'VE BEEN GUIDING YOUNG GODDESSES LIKE YOURSELF FOR THOUSANDS OF YEARS.
I CAN'T BELIEVE THAT ACTUALLY WORKED.
DUDE, MAX! I HAVE NO IDEA WHAT'S GOING ON, BUT YOU WERE SO DOPE!
ARE YOU ALL RIGHT? HOW ARE YOU FEELING?
JEN!
M-MY BINDER IS GONE!

Episode 5:
TROUBLES WITHIN

IT'S STILL NOT GOING AWAY, HUH? IT TURNED YOUR HAIR SILVER AND EVERYTHING...
Y'KNOW, THIS IS THE FIRST TIME I'VE EVER SEEN YOU IN A DRESS AND MAKEUP.
I KNOW! AND I CAN'T JUST TAKE IT OFF OR I'LL BE NAKED! UGH. I WANT TO RIP IT APART!
BUT IF I DID THAT, WOULD IT RIP MY CLOTHES WHEN I CHANGE BACK?
. . . .

YEAH. BEST LEAVE IT ALONE. BUT HEY, THE WAY YOU KEPT TRYIN' TO BEAT THAT MONSTER UP?
DIDN'T KNOW THERE WAS A FIGHTER IN YOU.
IT DIDN'T DO MUCH, THOUGH.
IT TOOK A GLORIFIED FLASHLIGHT TO GET RID OF IT.
HECK, MY DAD USED TO TEACH ME SELF-DEFENSE WHEN I WAS A KID. AND BY TEACH, I MEAN JUST THROWIN' ANYTHING AT ME TO BLOCK OR HIT.
RUB RUB
HE WAS CONVINCED IT WOULD KEEP ME SAFE, AND I WAS PRETTY GOOD AT IT. PLUS, IT GOT ME OUT OF BALLET CLASSES.
IF ONLY HE KNEW I WAS GOING TO BE DEALING WITH MON–

WAIT A MINUTE.
GASP!
HE WAS TOTALLY IN ON THIS, TOO!
PING
MY WHOLE LIFE IS A CONSPIRACY.
I'M FOREVER DESTINED TO BE SOME MAGICAL GIRL, FORCED TO FIGHT LIGHT-EATING MONSTERS WITH LIGHT.
...
THAT DOESN'T EVEN MAKE SENSE!

NAH, MAN, DON'T THINK OF IT LIKE THAT.
YOU'RE A MAGICAL BOY!
YOU KNOW...
JUST DRESSED IN DRAG...
AND CAPABLE OF SHOOTING LIGHT BEAMS FROM STICKS AND TALKING TO CATS.
OH, RIGHT! I'M STILL MAD AT YOU FOR HAVING ANYTHING TO DO WITH THIS!

HONESTLY, IT'S ABOUT TIME YOU CAN HEAR ME. I'VE BEEN WAITING FOR AGES!
AND FOR YOUR INFORMATION, MY NAME IS LORD—
AS IF IMMA CALL YOU THAT, YA WALNUT!
MEOW MEOW MEOW
WHAT'S HE SAYING?
WHAT? YOU CAN'T HEAR HIM?
OF COURSE NOT. ONLY ONES WITH THE GODDESS'S GIFT CAN HEAR ME.

IS HE, LIKE...YOUR LITTLE MASCOT NOW?
NO. HE'S JUST AN OLD FART THAT'S APPARENTLY BEEN FREELOADING OFF MY FAMILY FOR CENTURIES.
EXCUSE YOU! I AM YOUR GUARDIAN! HAVE SOME RESPECT.
OH, MAYBE HE KNOWS SOME THINGS.
ASK HIM ABOUT THAT BUG. LIKE, WHY DID IT SUDDENLY GET BIGGER AFTER EATING PYPER'S LIGHT? THAT WAS SCARY.
WAIT, DUDE. WHAT IF THE LIGHT YOU'RE SEEING IS OUR LIFE SOURCE?
I MEAN, LOOK AT HOW PYPER DROPPED AFTER SHE WAS ATTACKED.

WELL, SHE'S NOT ENTIRELY WRONG.

AS A DESCENDANT OF THE GODDESS, YOU ARE ABLE TO SEE THE ESSENCE OF ONE'S LIFE ENERGY. IT IS WITHIN ALL LIVING CREATURES.

THE GREAT GODDESS, AURORA, KEPT THIS ENERGY PURE WITH LOVE AND AFFECTION.

THE LIGHT OF THOSE SHE TOUCHED WOULD SHINE BRIGHTER THAN EVER WITH PEACE AND HAPPINESS.

THEN THERE WERE CREATURES OF THE DARK, MUCH LIKE YOU SAW HERE TODAY.

THEY FEED ON NEGATIVITY AND ARE WHAT YOU HUMANS LIKE TO CALL "SPIRITS."

THESE ARE ENTITIES THAT ARE CAPABLE OF BRINGING OUT THE WORST IN YOU, TAINTING YOUR LIGHT WITH MISERY AND FEAR.

THIS MAKES YOUR LIGHT VERY TOXIC AND POTENT, GIVING ANY DARK CREATURES OVERWHELMING POWER WHEN THEY CONSUME IT.
THEY'LL SUCK YOU DRY, WHEN GIVEN THE CHANCE, AND LEAVE YOU DRAINED LIKE A RAISIN.
AS A RESULT, THIS GIVES EVEN THE WEAKEST PEST THE ABILITY TO BECOME THE MOST MENACING BEAST.
MEOW MEOW MEOW MEOW
SQUEEE!
WHAT'S HE SAYING?
SNAP SNAP
OH, UHH... BAD BUGS EAT THE LIGHT FARTS AND GET BLOATED?
HISSSS
HOW UNDIGNIFIED! THAT'S NOT WHAT I SAID AT ALL!

WELL, WHAT YOU SAID WAS LONG AND BORING!
MEOW MEOW MEOW
MMMMM
OH, SHUT IT.
WHAT HAPPENED? WHERE AM I?
AND WHAT DID YOU DO TO ME?
WHAT?! WE DIDN'T DO ANYTHING.
WE JUST SAVED YOUR BUTT FROM A FREAKIN' MONSTER. YOU SHOULD BE THANKING US!
SAVED ME?
RAHH

I-I DON'T KNOW WHAT YOU'RE TALKING ABOUT.
WHO THE HECK IS THIS?
THE PERSON WHO SAVED YOU!
OH GOOD, SHE DOESN'T RECOGNIZE ME.

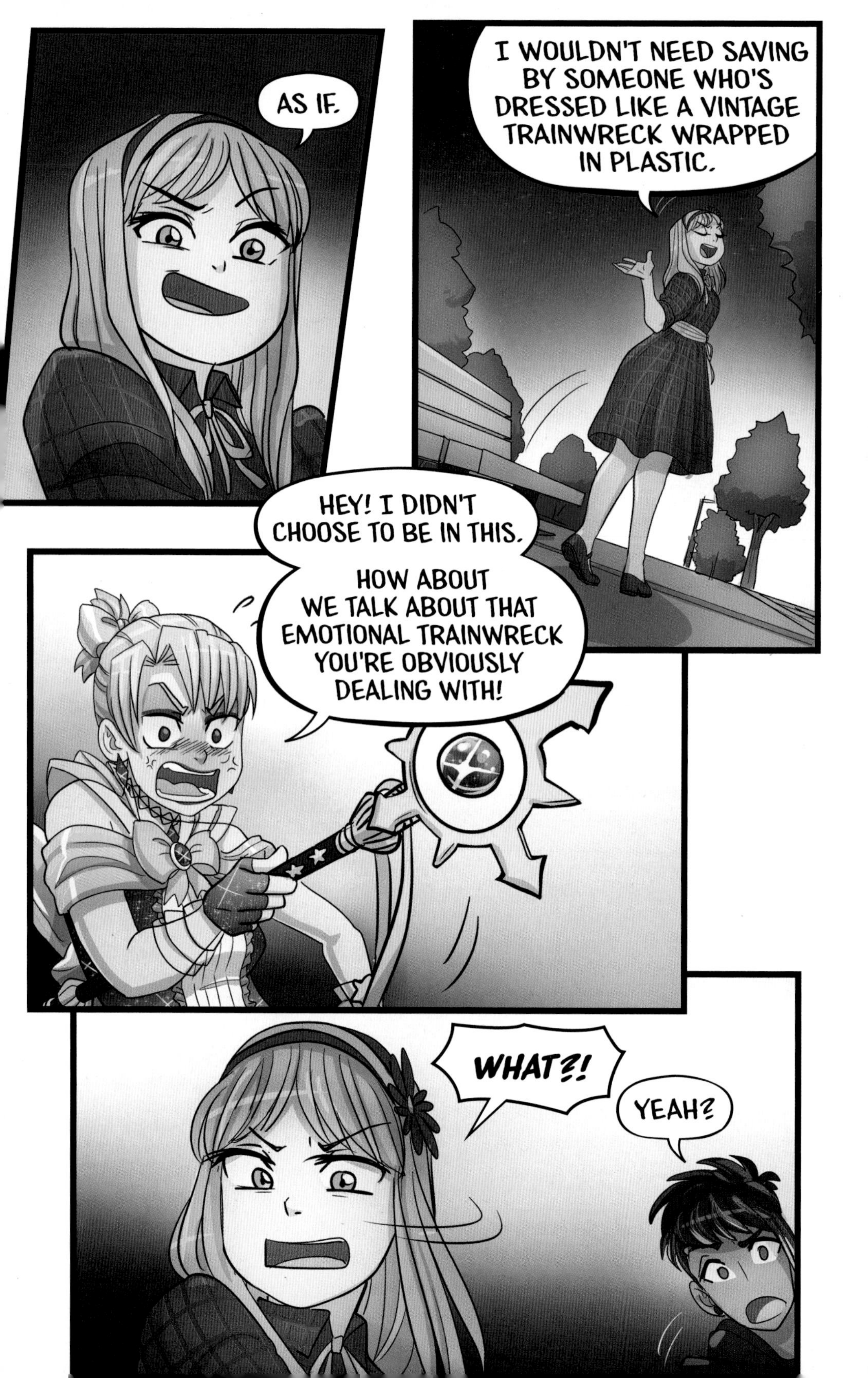
AS IF.
I WOULDN'T NEED SAVING BY SOMEONE WHO'S DRESSED LIKE A VINTAGE TRAINWRECK WRAPPED IN PLASTIC.
HEY! I DIDN'T CHOOSE TO BE IN THIS.
HOW ABOUT WE TALK ABOUT THAT EMOTIONAL TRAINWRECK YOU'RE OBVIOUSLY DEALING WITH!
WHAT?!
YEAH?

I MEAN... IT WAS YOUR LEVEL OF REPRESSED EMOTIONS THAT SPAWNED A RHINO-SIZED BEAST.
SO... WHAT'S REALLY GOING ON, PYPER?
WHY ARE YOU SO FILLED WITH ANGER THAT YOU'RE ALWAYS PICKING ON US... ER...JEN LIKE AN OBSESSION?
YEAH!
BECAUSE BEING GAY IS WRONG!
WHOA
JEN AND EVERYONE LIKE HER ARE JUST FLAUNTING THEMSELVES RIGHT OUT IN THE OPEN!
IT'S A DISGRACE TO EVERYTHING THAT I—
Hey!

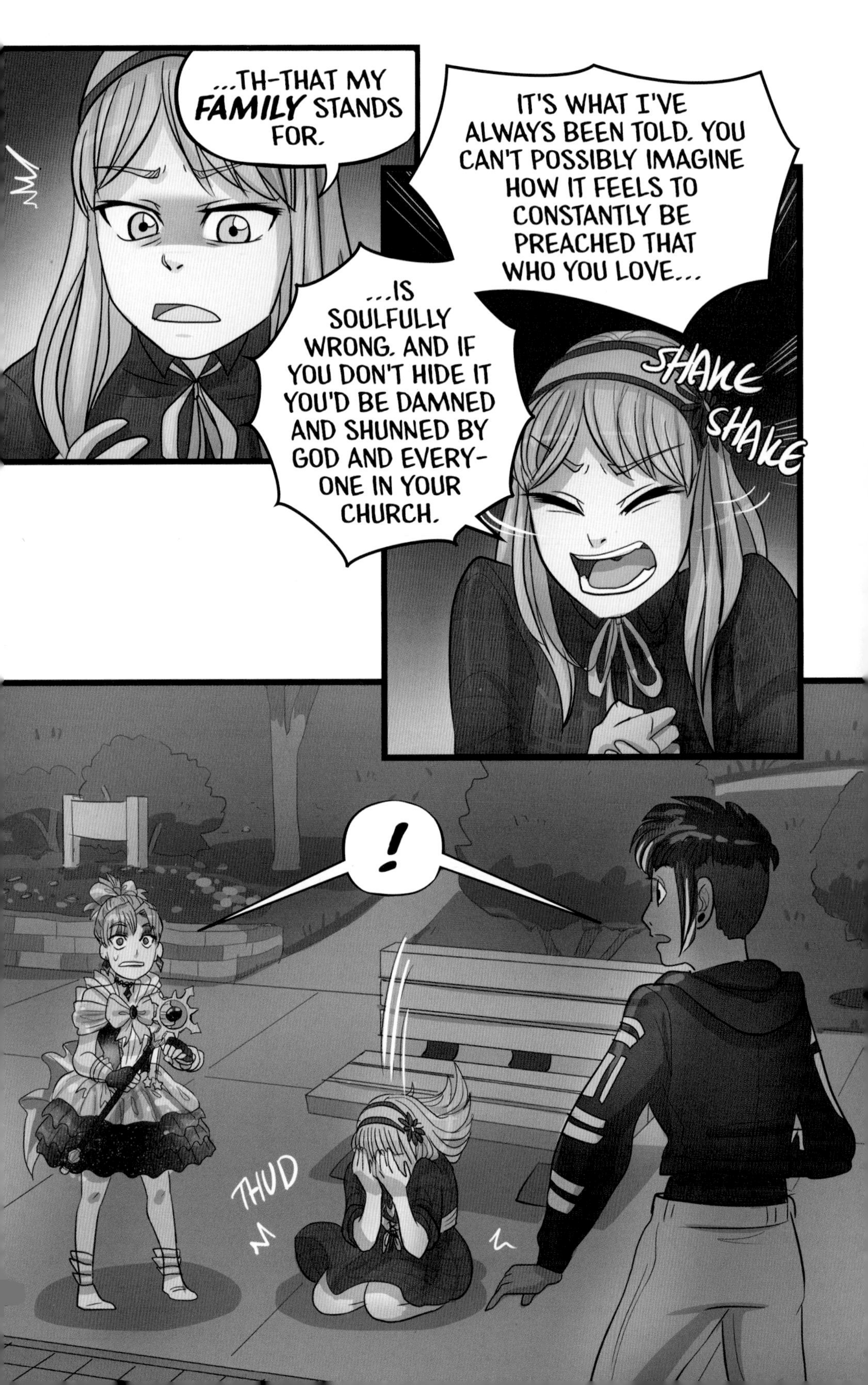
...TH-THAT MY **FAMILY** STANDS FOR.
IT'S WHAT I'VE ALWAYS BEEN TOLD. YOU CAN'T POSSIBLY IMAGINE HOW IT FEELS TO CONSTANTLY BE PREACHED THAT WHO YOU LOVE...
...IS SOULFULLY WRONG. AND IF YOU DON'T HIDE IT YOU'D BE DAMNED AND SHUNNED BY GOD AND EVERY-ONE IN YOUR CHURCH.
SHAKE
SHAKE
!
THUD

I TRIED SO HARD TO SUPPRESS IT SINCE THE DAY YOU CAME OUT TO ME.
!
I WAS SO HAPPY TO LEARN...

...I WASN'T ALONE.

CHU

BUT IT WAS STILL WRONG, AND I COULDN'T LET MY FAMILY DOWN.

BUT WHO AM I KIDDING?
GOD SEES RIGHT THROUGH ME AND IS PUNISHING ME.
HUH, THE DARK CREATURES DON'T HAVE TO DO MUCH, YOU HUMANS ARE ALREADY A HOT MESS.
EASY FUEL FOR THEM
SHUSH!
AYE THERE... UH...BUDDY?
IT'S NOT WHAT YOU THINK. THESE MONSTERS AREN'T HERE TO PUNISH YOU.

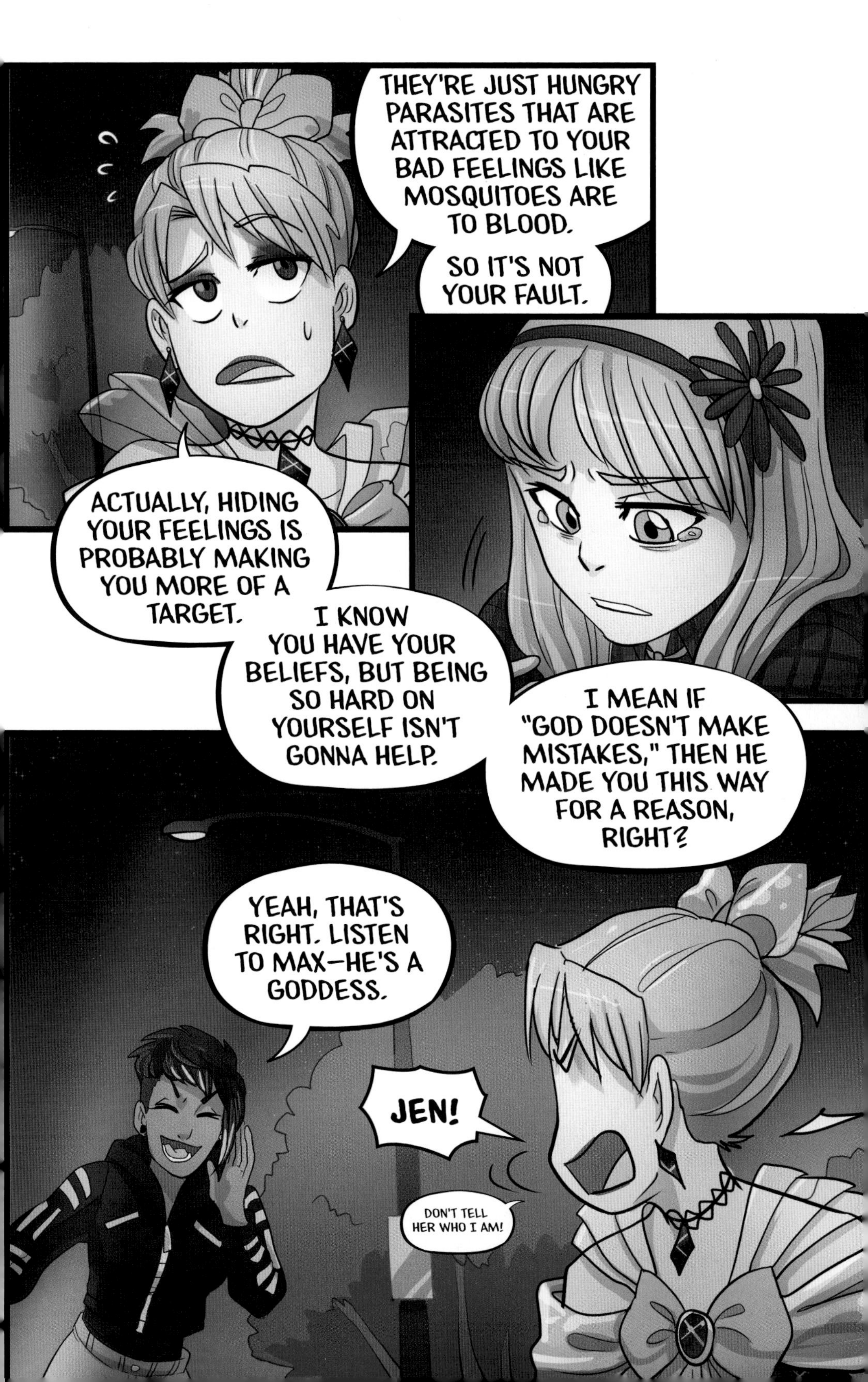
THEY'RE JUST HUNGRY PARASITES THAT ARE ATTRACTED TO YOUR BAD FEELINGS LIKE MOSQUITOES ARE TO BLOOD.
SO IT'S NOT YOUR FAULT.
ACTUALLY, HIDING YOUR FEELINGS IS PROBABLY MAKING YOU MORE OF A TARGET.
I KNOW YOU HAVE YOUR BELIEFS, BUT BEING SO HARD ON YOURSELF ISN'T GONNA HELP.
I MEAN IF "GOD DOESN'T MAKE MISTAKES," THEN HE MADE YOU THIS WAY FOR A REASON, RIGHT?
YEAH, THAT'S RIGHT. LISTEN TO MAX—HE'S A GODDESS.
JEN!
DON'T TELL HER WHO I AM!

OH MY GOD.
AM I BEING CONVERTED?
IS THIS THE GAY AGENDA?
YES.
WHAT? NO!
THIS IS IT. I AM BEING CONVERTED BY A LESBIAN GODDESS.

WHOA, I AM NOT A LESBIAN OR A GODDESS. I AM A MAN!
THAT'S IT. I'M GOING TO HELL.
HEY, CHILL. DON'T WORRY ABOUT IT. I'LL TALK TO HER AND GET HER HOME.
SIGH. HERE IT GOES.
DING DONG
I THINK YOU MIGHT WANNA HEAD HOME, TOO.
YOU'RE GONNA HAVE TO MAKE UP WITH YOUR MOM AND FIGURE THIS THING OUT.
AH CRAP, YOU'RE RIGHT.
GOOD LUCK!

WHERE HAVE YOU BE–
AHHH
HIKARI, IS EVERYTHING OKAY?
KAI, SHE DID IT! SHE DID HER FIRST TRANSFORMATION!

IT LOOKS JUST LIKE MY OLD OUTFIT BACK IN THE EARLY '90s.
DOES THIS MEAN YOU HAD TO CONFRONT ONE OF THOSE THINGS? ARE YOU OKAY, ?
OF COURSE SHE IS—LOOK AT HER!
WHAT DID I TELL YOU?! IT'S NOT JUST A STORY! NOW, WERE YOU ABLE TO SEAL UP THE LEAK PROPERLY?
LEAK? WHAT LEAK?
WHAT?!
YOU DIDN'T FIX THE LEAK? WHENEVER THERE'S A MONSTER, THERE'S ALWAYS A CRACK IN THE SEAL NEARBY!

AS DESCENDANTS OF THE GODDESS, IT IS OUR DUTY TO PROTECT THE SEAL!
YOU KNOW, THE ONLY THING THAT IS KEEPING THE DARK KING FROM BREAKING BACK INTO THIS REALM!
WALNUT, WHY DIDN'T YOU MENTION ANYTHING ABOUT THIS?
YOU WERE TOO BUSY CONSULTING YOUR HUMAN FRIEND.
HONESTLY, YOU SHOULD HAVE ALREADY KNOWN ABOUT ALL THIS. DIDN'T YOUR MOTHER READ YOU THE BOOK?
I WAS JUST A KID! NO ONE IN THEIR RIGHT MIND WOULD TAKE THAT STORY SERIOUSLY.
DON'T FRET, THE CREATURE WAS A SMALL-TIMER.
WE CAN EASILY GO BACK FIRST THING IN THE MORNING TO PATCH THE LEAK UP. FOR NOW, JUST GET SOME REST. YOU WILL NEED IT.
SMALL-TIMER?! DID YOU SEE THE SIZE OF THAT THING?

YOU CAN HEAR WALNUT NOW?
YEAH, THANKS FOR THE HEADS-UP!
WHY DIDN'T YOU TELL ME ABOUT HIM?
OH, HONEY, IT WOULDN'T HAVE MATTERED IF YOU NEVER DEVELOPED YOUR POWERS.
EVER SINCE YOU WERE BORN, I WAS NO LONGER ABLE TO HEAR HIM. IT'S BEEN SO LONG I NEARLY FORGOT.
WHAT DID HE SAY?
SERIOUSLY?

UGH.
IT'S MAX!
AND HE SAID WE'LL TAKE CARE OF IT TOMORROW. I'M GOING TO BED!
STOMP
STOMP
STOMP
THIS SUCKS!
FWUMP

POOF
OH SWEET MANGOES, YES. MY BINDER IS BACK!

Episode 6:
TAKING INITIATIVE

03:59 AM
04:00 AM
RISE AND SHINE, !

WHAT THE HECK? IT'S NOT EVEN 7:00 YET.
04:00 AM
THERE'S NO TIME TO LOSE!
I HAVE TO TEACH YOU HOW TO PROPERLY TRANSFORM BEFORE YOU PATCH UP THE LEAK.
YANK
CAN'T WE DO THIS AFTER SCHOOL?
ABSOLUTELY NOT. THE MORE WE WAIT, THE MORE UNSTABLE THE SEAL WILL GET!

AS DESCENDANTS OF THE GODDESS AURORA, WE CANNOT LET THAT HAPPEN!
WELL, IF YOU DO IT AFTER YOUR EDUCATION, WHEN MORE HUMANS ARE PRESENT, YOU'LL BE RECOGNIZED FOR THE HARD WORK YOU'RE DOING FOR THE WORLD.
THEN AGAIN, HUMANS LACK THE ABILITY TO SEE THESE WEAK CREATURES AND LEAKS.
YOU'LL JUST LOOK INSANE TO THEM.
YOU KNOW WHAT, YOU'RE RIGHT. THE EARLIER THE BETTER.
LET'S GET THIS OVER WITH.

AS YOU KNOW...
IT WAS THE POWERS OF AURORA THAT SEALED THE NASTY KING AND ALL HIS EVIL LITTLE MINIONS INTO ANOTHER REALM...
KEEPING US AND EVERYONE ELSE SAFE FROM THEM.
WITH EACH NEW GENERATION, THE SEAL WEAKENS. LITTLE CRACKS START TO APPEAR, WHICH ALLOW THE SMALLEST MINIONS TO SQUEEZE INTO OUR REALM—HENCE WHY WE CALL THEM LEAKS.
THE LONGER A LEAK IS LEFT UNTREATED, THE MORE CREATURES YOU'LL HAVE TO CLEAN UP AFTER.

NOT ONLY WILL THEY CAUSE HAVOC FROM TAINTING AND CONSUMING HUMAN LIGHT, BUT THEY'LL ALSO BECOME POWERFUL ENOUGH TO CREATE LARGER LEAKS.
YOU MUST STOP THEM BEFORE THAT HAPPENS.
WHICH IS WHY IT'S VERY IMPORTANT TO PATCH THESE LEAKS RIGHT AWAY. WE NEED TO PREVENT THE INFESTATION AS MUCH AS POSSIBLE!
BUT, OF COURSE, IN ORDER TO DO THAT YOU'LL NEED TO BE ABLE TO TRANSFORM WITH EASE.
I EXPECT IT MIGHT TAKE YOU SOME TIME TO GET USED TO, BEING A LATE BLOOMER AND ALL.
WHICH IS WHY WE'RE HERE.

LATE BLOOMER?
FOR YOUR INFORMATION, I TRANSFORMED PERFECTLY FINE LAST NIGHT.
HOW HARD CAN IT BE TO DO IT AGAIN?
I WAS ONLY THIRTEEN WHEN I DEVELOPED MY ABILITIES, AND IT TOOK ME YEARS TO PERFECT THE ART OF TRANSFORMING.
WHOOSH
WHOOSH

WHAT ON EARTH ARE YOU DOING?
THIS IS EXACTLY WHAT I WAS AFRAID OF. YOU CAN'T JUST FLAIL AROUND LIKE A BABOON!
YOU NEED TO PERSONALIZE YOUR APPEARANCE AND MOVEMENTS IN THE IMAGE AND GRACE OF A GODDESS.
IT'S ONLY THEN THAT YOU'LL BECOME ONE WITH AURORA.
I'M PRETTY SURE I WASN'T PRANCING AROUND AND POSING LIKE A DELICATE FLOWER WHEN I TRANSFORMED.
IT WAS PROBABLY JUST... WHAT DO YOU HUMANS CALL IT?
BEGINNER'S LUCK?
SHUT UP. I CAN DO IT AGAIN.

WAHHH
HAHHHH!

POOF
WHAT WAS THAT?
ARE YOU TRYING TO MAKE A FOOL OUT OF YOURSELF?
STOP MESSING AROUND, . THIS IS SERIOUS.
YOU NEED TO START ACTING LIKE A LADY!

WE'VE BEEN THROUGH THIS! I'M NOT A LADY.
AND MY NAME IS MAX.
THIS AGAIN?
JUST DO WHAT YOUR MOTHER SAYS. I MEAN, HOW CAN YOU KNOW IF YOU NEVER TRY BEING MORE LADYLIKE?
YOU KNOW WHAT? FINE. I'LL DO THE STUPID POSES.

WELL, THIS IS A START.
DON'T TELL ME I HAVE TO ADD A DUMB CATCHPHRASE TO GO WITH IT, LIKE...
"FROM THE GODDESS OF AURORA, LET THERE BE LIGHT!"
OF COURSE NOT...
YOU HAVE TO SAY IT WITH MORE SOUL!

OKAY, THIS ISN'T WORKING. I QUIT.
NO, NO, I'M JOKING!
THOUGH IT DOES HELP. JUST SAYING.
TRY AGAIN. THIS TIME, FOCUS ON BREATHING.
INHALE
...
EXHALE

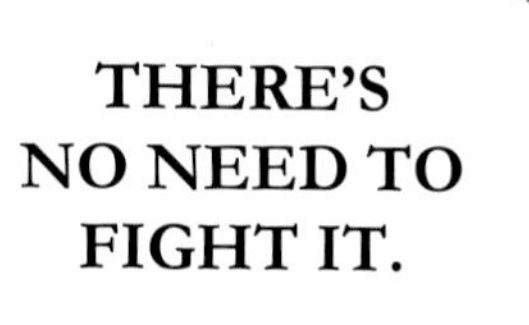

LET IT FLOW, AND IT WILL COME TO YOU.

AHHHHH!
WHAT HAPPENED?! ARE WE UNDER ATTACK?
NO, NO, IT'S ONLY . SHE SUCCESSFULLY TRANSFORMED AGAIN!
OH... AT THIS HOUR?
I'M NEVER GOING TO GET USED TO THIS.

NOW GO FIND THAT LEAK. WALNUT WILL GUIDE YOU.
I DON'T WANNA!
GOOD LUCK! CALL ME WHEN YOU'RE DONE.
YOU DIDN'T EVEN TEACH ME HOW TO DO IT!
SLAM
IT'S NOT THAT HARD. COME ALONG NOW.

BUBBLE TEA HOUSE
HOW DO YOU EVEN KNOW WHERE TO LOOK?
IT'S MY LIFELONG DUTY TO GUARD THE SEAL. IF THERE'S A LEAK, I'LL KNOW ABOUT IT.
AH! IT'S THAT BUG THING!
QUICK, DISPOSE OF IT WITH YOUR STAFF.
PEW!

HISSS
HUH, THAT WAS EASY.
DON'T GET DISTRACTED NOW. THERE'S MORE. WE'RE GETTING CLOSE.

EASY-PEASY.
PEW
PEW
PEW
ZAP
ZAP
ZAP
HISSSSS

HEY, THAT ONE LOOKED DIFFERENT.
NO MATTER, THEY ARE ALL THE SAME. ONLY THE WEAK ARE SMALL ENOUGH TO SLIP THROUGH THE SEAL'S CRACK.
AT THEIR CURRENT STATE, THEY CAN ONLY TAKE THE SHAPE OF LOWER LIFE-FORMS.
BUT, OF COURSE, AS YOU WITNESSED LAST NIGHT, THEY CAN EVENTUALLY BECOME BIGGER AND INCREDIBLY ANNOYING.
OH YEAH, ABOUT THAT.
HOW COME THE OTHERS HAD TROUBLE SEEING IT WHEN IT WAS LITTLE?
PEW
HAVEN'T YOU BEEN LISTENING TO ME?

THEY'RE LIKE SPIRITS—INVISIBLE TO THE HUMAN EYE UNTIL THEY CONSUME ENOUGH TAINTED LIGHT.
THE DENSE TOXIC ENERGY ALLOWS THEM TO DEVELOP NOT ONLY POWER, BUT ALSO A STRONGER PRESENCE TO BE SEEN IN THIS REALM.
GOT IT. THE FATTER THEY ARE, THE EASIER IT IS FOR PEOPLE TO SEE THEM.
THAT'S NOT WHAT I SAID!
AH, I THINK I SEE IT!

WIGGLE
WIGGLE
OH NO YOU DON'T. GET BACK IN THERE.
THUD
THIS IS IT. IN ORDER TO REPAIR THE LEAK, YOU'LL NEED TO—
GET A ROLL OF DUCT TAPE.
WHAT? NO.

STOP IT WITH YOUR NONSENSE.
YOU USE THE POWER FROM YOUR AMULET BY ALIGNING THE STAFF WITH IT.
LIKE THIS?
SHIING
!

VERY GOOD. NOW, GENTLY WAVE—
I GOT THIS.
GRIP

ARE YOU INSANE?!
WH
AM!

WHOOOSH
ZIP
AH...
I DID IT.
THAT SHOULDN'T HAVE WORKED.
POOF

IT WAS UNNECESSARILY AGGRESSIVE.
WHOA!
POOF
DAMN IT. OF COURSE IT DISAPPEARS SUDDENLY NOW.
I SHOULD HAVE GOTTEN DRESSED BEFORE THIS.
COME GET ME MOM!
TIK
TIK
TIK

WHOOO
OOSHH
REALLY?
ode 7:
E ME
A MAN

RING
RING
RING
THUNK
I'M SO TIRED.
YOU ALL RIGHT? DIDN'T SEE YOU IN HOMEROOM.
CHATTER
CHATTER
CHATTER
CHATTER
CHATTER CHATTER
FWOMP
YEAH, I WAS LATE EVEN THOUGH I'VE BEEN UP SINCE 4:00 A.M. MY MOM HAD ME TRANSFORM INTO THAT HORRIBLE POOFY AND SPARKLY OUTFIT AGAIN TO DO MORE GODDESS-DESCENDANT WORK,
AND NOW I'VE GOTTA CARRY THIS DUMB THING AROUND. I DON'T KNOW WHERE TO PUT IT AND I SURE AS HELL AIN'T GONNA WEAR IT.
HA HA HA

OH, HANG ON. MAYBE I CAN HELP.
SNICKER
SNICKER
IS IT JUST ME, OR ARE PEOPLE STARING?
TAP
CLICK
TAP
WELL, THIS IS THE FIRST TIME PEOPLE ARE SEEING YOUR HAIR—
, YOU'RE NOT ALLOWED TO HAVE YOUR HOOD UP INSIDE. ARE YOU ALREADY ASHAMED OF YOUR BUTCH HAIRCUT?
HAVING SECOND THOUGHTS ABOUT COMING OUT AS GAY?
WHAT?
STOP TRYING TO HIDE IT. WE ALREADY CONFRONTED YOU LAST NIGHT AT THE BUBBLE TEA HOUSE.
YEAH, THEY TOTALLY SNUCK OUT AFTER WE CAUGHT THEM. PROBABLY WENT OFF TO DO THE UNSPEAKABLE.
C'MON, GIRLS, DON'T WASTE YOUR BREATH ON THEM.
THEY CAN'T BE SERIOUS.
RIGHT. THEY'RE NOT WORTH OUR TIME.

WHAT WAS THAT?
WHERE'D YOU GO LAST NIGHT?
NOTHING. HERE'S YOUR NECKLACE.
WHAT DO YOU THINK?
I TURNED IT INTO A BRACELET.
IT'S STILL A BIT FLASHY BUT AT LEAST IT'S NOT TOO FEMININE ANYMORE.
AH! IT'S PERFECT!

COOL BRACELET, ████.
INTRODUCING THE CLASS PRESIDENT, TOBI.
T-TOBI?!
HE'S SUPER NICE, CUTE, AND ALWAYS HAS THIS PEACEFUL GREEN LIGHT AROUND HIM THAT CALMS ME DOWN.
HEY. SORRY, I COULDN'T HELP BUT OVERHEAR. DON'T LET PYPER AND HER GANG GET TO YOU.
A HAIRCUT IS JUST A FASHION CHOICE, AND THE NEW ONE REALLY SUITS YOU.
YEAH, IT MAKES YOU LOOK LIKE A DUDE!
WELL JOKE'S ON YOU! THAT'S WHAT I WAS GOING FOR!
OH, REALLY?
AH, Y-YEAH... I MEAN...
TOTALLY! IT REALLY SUITS HIM, RIGHT? HE GOES BY MAX NOW.
JEN!

HAHA, I'M ACTUALLY NOT SURPRISED. IT'S FITTING REALLY.
Y-YOU THINK SO?
YEAH, ESPECIALLY HOW YOU CARRY YOURSELF.
ANYWAYS, I GOTTA RUN TO THE LIBRARY. SEE YOU LATER, MAX. LATER, JEN.
WHAT WERE YOU THINKING?!
HEY, I WAS JUST FOLLOWING THROUGH FROM WHAT YOU SAID!
PAP
I MEAN, TECHNICALLY I DIDN'T OUTRIGHT TELL HIM THAT YOU'RE TRANS, AND HE TOOK WHAT WE TOLD HIM REALLY WELL.
HE DID CALL ME MAX...DID THAT REALLY JUST HAPPEN?
YO, WE SHOULD CELEBRATE!

LET'S GET YOU SOME NEW CLOTHES TO MATCH YOUR NEW LOOK.
HEH, ARE YOU EXCITED THAT YOU'RE GETTING CLOSER TO YOUR CRUSH?
SHUSH! TOBI ISN'T EVEN INTO GUYS.
MAYBE HE'LL MAKE AN EXCEPTION FOR YOU.
WHAT? NO! THAT MEANS HE'D STILL SEE ME AS A WOMAN, AND I DON'T WANT THAT.
I'M A MAN, AND I'D WANT TO DATE SOMEONE WHO SEES ME AS ONE. BUT WHAT IF I'M NOT ACCEPTED AS A GAY MAN?
WELL, TOBI COULD BE BI. WE DON'T KNOW.
IF A GUY DOESN'T ACCEPT YOU FOR WHO YOU ARE, THEN THEY DON'T DESERVE YOU IN THE FIRST PLACE.
HERE, TRY THESE ON.
Hmm

THIS SHOWS OFF YOUR CURVES TOO MUCH.
HELLO, SIR, DID YOU FIND EVERYTHING YOU NEED ALL RIGHT?
WHAT? ARE YOU TALKING TO ME?
OH, I'M SORRY, MA'AM. YES, DO YOU NEED ANY HELP WITH ANYTHING?
NO, I'M GOOD.
HOW ABOUT YOU, MA'AM?
OH, COME ON!
HAHA, SORRY. WE'RE GOOD.
HERE, MAX. TRY THIS ONE.
SINCE YOU LIKE HOODIES, HERE'S SOME DIFFERENT OPTIONS.

OOOH! THIS IS COMFY.
I LIKE HOW THIS VEST ANGLES OUT MY SHOULDERS.
HEHE. I LIKE THIS HOODIE!
AWESOME! LET'S TAKE THEM ALL.
WAIT, WHAT?

JEN, YOU REALLY DIDN'T HAVE TO GET ME THESE. HOW CAN YOU EVEN AFFORD ALL THIS?
HONESTLY, YOU'VE BEEN WEARING THE SAME OLD YELLOW HOODIE. IT WAS ABOUT TIME FOR AN INTERVENTION.
HEY, IT WAS THE ONLY BAGGY THING I MANAGED TO GET MY MOM TO BUY ME.
EXACTLY. DON'T YOU FEEL BETTER IN THIS NEW OUTFIT?
OF COURSE! I CAN'T THANK YOU ENOUGH.
THOUGH, I'M STILL KINDA SALTY THAT THE SALES REP THOUGHT YOU WERE A GUY AND NOT ME.
HAHA. YEAH, MISGENDERING DOESN'T HELP ANYONE.
RIGHT...IT'S PROBABLY REALLY ANNOYING FOR YOU TO GET MISTAKEN AS A GUY.
OH, LOOK!

THEY OPENED UP THAT NEW KAWAII CLOUD STORE! THEY HAVE ALL THOSE SUPER-CUTE COLLECTIBLE THINGIES IN THERE. LET'S GO CHECK IT OUT.
UGH, DO WE HAVE TO?
C'MON, GOING IN THERE AIN'T GONNA TAINT YOUR MASCULINITY.
I-I KNOW THAT!
WAIT FOR M—
BUMP
DUDE, WATCH WHERE YOU'RE GOING!
PA-TUU

YOU OKAY?
DID YOU SEE THAT? HE CALLED ME "DUDE" AND LOOKED LIKE HE WANTED TO FIGHT ME!
Y'KNOW, GETTING INTO A FIGHT IS NOT SOMETHING YOU SHOULD BE EXCITED ABOUT...
THAT WAS SEAN MOORE. HE GOES TO OUR SCHOOL. I HEARD HE'S REALLY BAD NEWS.
I KNOW YOU ALREADY BEAT THAT MONSTER NOT TOO LONG AGO...
BUT IT'S BEST NOT TO GET YOURSELF INTO MORE TROUBLE FOR NO REASON.
YOU SHOULD BE MORE CAREFUL.

Episode 8:
HOW'S IT GOING TO BE?

CREAK
WHERE HAVE YOU BEEN? YOU WERE SUPPOSED TO COME HOME STRAIGHT AFTER SCHOOL TO TRAIN MORE.
click
AND WHAT IS THIS? WHAT ARE YOU WEARING?

WHERE DID YOUR BOOBS GO?!
IT'S JUST CLOTHES!
THIS IS NO TIME TO BE MASKING YOUR FEMININITY WITH THOSE BOYISH CLOTHES!
STOMP
STOMP
LOOK, CAN YOU JUST LET ME WEAR WHAT I WANT AND I'LL PROMISE TO TRAIN MORE?
I'M GOING TO BE TRANSFORMING INTO A DIFFERENT OUTFIT ANYWAYS. DOES IT REALLY MATTER WHAT I WEAR OUTSIDE OF THIS?
I DON'T THINK YOU UNDERSTAND THE SIT–

I SAY GO FOR IT.
PAT
WHAT ARE YOU DOING?
C'MON, HIKARI, IT'S A GOOD COMPROMISE.
I GUESS THIS IS BETTER THAN HER RESISTING COMPLETELY.
ALL RIGHT, FINE.
BUT YOU'LL HAVE TO TRAIN RIGHT NOW BEFORE YOU GO TO BED TONIGHT.
!
R-REALLY? OKAY.
YAY! I GET TO WEAR BAGGY CLOTHES MORE FREELY.
CAN YOU TRANSFORM LIKE YOU DID THIS MORNING?

HONESTLY, YOU'RE ONLY MAKING IT MORE DIFFICULT ON YOURSELF WITH THIS NEW LOOK.
I CAN DO IT.
INHALE
HYAHH!
!
PAT
...

WELL DONE.
WHOOSHHH
HUH?
AW MAN, CAN'T I KEEP THE BINDER ON?

PING
GASP!
OH, I CAN ACTUALLY BREATHE AGAIN.
PING
MAYBE WEARING THAT ALL DAY LONG ISN'T SUCH A GOOD IDEA...

WHOOOO OOSH!
!
HEY, IS IT JUST ME OR IS THE OUTFIT A LITTLE DIFFERENT?

THAT'S TO BE EXPECTED.
IT EVOLVES WITH EACH AND EVERY GENERATION AS THEY GROW AND MATURE INTO THEIR OWN GODDESS-LIKE IMAGE.
WELL THEN, I'LL LET YOU TWO GET ON WITH IT.
I'LL GO MAKE SOME DINNER.
WAIT, DOES THAT MEAN THERE'S A CHANCE I CAN TURN THIS INTO PANTS?
OF COURSE NOT. HISTORICALLY, THEY HAVE ALWAYS BEEN BEAUTIFUL GOWNS.
UGH, THAT'S STUPID. HOW ARE THESE POOFY DRESSES EVEN PRACTICAL? THEY FLY UP IN ALL DIRECTIONS AND GET CAUGHT ON THINGS.
IT WON'T IF YOU CARRY YOURSELF PROPERLY.

IN FACT, LET'S GET TO WORK ON YOUR POSES FOR OFFENSIVE MOVES.
SIMPLY SWINGING THE STAFF AROUND WILL NOT BE AS EFFECTIVE AS PUTTING GRACE AND ELEGANCE INTO IT.
IT'S BEEN WORKING FINE FOR ME SO FAR.
WIELDING THE GODDESS'S POWER WITH AGGRESSION IS IMPROPER, UNPREDICTABLE, CHAOTIC, AND UNRELIABLE!
YOU NEED TO DO WHAT HAS ALWAYS WORKED.
WHOOOOSH
FOR EXAMPLE! WITH A MORE MINDFUL AND FLUID MOTION, LIKE A BALLERINA...
SWISHH
YOU'LL BE PUTTING THE CORRECT BALANCED ENERGY OF PURITY AND PEACE INTO YOUR EXECUTION.
YOUR ATTACKS WILL BECOME STRONGER, STURDIER, AND MORE POWERFUL.
NOW YOU TRY IT. AIM AT THIS PLANT.
WON'T THE PLANT EXPLODE IF I HIT IT?

OF COURSE NOT. THIS IS AURORA'S LIGHT WE'RE TALKING ABOUT.
IT SHOULD ONLY MAKE THE PLANT'S LIFE ENERGY THRIVE. NOW, COME ON.
BOOM
ALL RIGHT. ALL RIGHT.
STEP
STEP
THIS IS SAD.
YOU LOOK LIKE A MONKEY IN A DRESS.
TWIRL
THEN DON'T WATCH!
WHOOSH
BLURP
THIS IS EXACTLY WHAT I FEARED.
THAT'S WHAT HAPPENS WHEN YOU DON'T EMBRACE YOUR WOMANHOOD.
YOU KNOW WHAT?
THIS IS ALL BECAUSE YOU KEEP HANGING OUT WITH THAT FRIEND OF YOURS. JEN, WAS IT?
HER BOYISH LOOKS AND PERSONALITY ARE RUBBING OFF ON YOU TOO MUCH.

WHOA!
YOU CAN'T CHANGE WHO I AM.
THIS HAS NOTHING TO DO WITH HER!
I GOT RID OF THE MONSTERS AND CLOSED UP THAT LEAK JUST FINE THIS MORNING.
ALL MY OWN WAY.
CLEARLY, YOUR WAY ISN'T WORKING FOR ME!
CLEARLY?! WELL, IF YOU'RE SO SURE OF YOURSELF, THEN PLEASE...
PROVE TO ME HOW GREAT YOUR WAY IS!
FINE, I WILL!
BZZZZ
BZZZ
POP

BOOSH
WHAT THE—?!
DON'T YOU SEE, ? THERE'S SO MUCH YOU DON'T KNOW.
JUST ACCEPT YOUR FATE AND LET ME HELP YOU!
OH NO, WHAT HAPPENED?
DASH
KNOCK
KNOCK
GO AWAY!

I HAVE A PEACE OFFERING. A LOADED POTATO CASSEROLE.
CREAK
HEY, I KNOW THINGS ARE HARD FOR YOU RIGHT NOW.
JUST KNOW I ONLY WANT WHAT'S BEST FOR YOU AND FOR YOU TO BE HAPPY.
IF THAT MEANS BECOMING A BOY, THEN SO BE IT.
CHOKE
WHAT? REALLY?
YES, OF COURSE, .
NOW WHEN IT COMES TO YOUR MOTHER, SHE REALLY DOES CARE ABOUT YOU.
IT'S MAX.
OH? MAX OWEN, HUH?
I LIKE IT.
SHE'S JUST AFRAID. SHE'S TRYING TO PREPARE YOU THE ONLY WAY SHE KNOWS HOW.
I ADMIT I'M STILL NOT SURE HOW THIS ALL WORKS.

THEY'RE OBVIOUSLY DOING SOMETHING WRONG IF THE SEAL KEEPS LEAKING.
THEY'VE BEEN DOING A GREAT JOB KEEPING THIS KING OF DARKNESS FROM TAKING OVER.
AND IF THEY WERE ABLE TO DO IT, SO CAN YOU!
AFTER ALL, SHE'S THE ONE WHO IS EXPERIENCED, AND I JUST WANT YOU TO BE SAFE.
THIS WON'T BE FOR FOREVER. I'M CONFIDENT YOU'LL GET THROUGH THIS. I MEAN, LOOK AT YOUR MOTHER NOW.
SHE'S LIVING OUT HER LIFE THE WAY SHE WANTS, MAGIC-FREE.
JUST HANG IN THERE AND REMEMBER I WILL ALWAYS BE HERE FOR YOU.
THANKS, DAD. LOVE YOU.
LOVE YOU TOO, HONEY.
PLEASE DON'T CALL ME THAT.
OKAY, BUN BUN.
DAD!
C'MON.
YOU'RE STILL MY LITTLE BABY.
ALL RIGHT, ALL RIGHT. GET SOME REST NOW, MAX.

NIGHT.
SHUT
FLOP
...
SMACK
THUNK
LEFT UNTREATED DEVOID WILL RETURN!

EPISODE 9:

UNAVOIDABLE

ARCADE
THANKS FOR HANGING OUT WITH ME AGAIN.
OF COURSE.
PING
CLICK
CLACK
AREN'T YOU GONNA GET IN TROUBLE FOR NOT GOING HOME TO TRAIN LIKE YOU PROMISED?
I ONLY PROMISED I'D TRAIN MORE.
IF I'M GOING TO BE FORCED INTO THIS, I'LL DO IT ON MY OWN TERMS.
PEW PEW PEW
OH SNAP.

I STILL DON'T UNDERSTAND WHY IT EVEN MATTERS WHAT I WEAR OR WHAT POSE I DO. IT DOESN'T MAKE SENSE!
YOU SAW ME BEAT THAT MONSTER JUST FINE WITHOUT PRANCING AROUND. UGH.
DAMN IT
ARGH NOO!
BAM
YEAH, YEAH. THAT'S WEIRD.
MAN, IS IT ME OR IS EVERYONE HERE IN A BAD MOOD?
HAHA! THIS IS TOO EASY. ONE EASY SLIP IN THESE CONTRAPTIONS...
AND THEY'RE DROWNING IN ANGER.

Y-YEAH, LET'S STAY CLEAR OF THEM.
IMMA TRY PLAYING THAT GAME OVER THERE.
I REALLY DON'T WANT TO DEAL WITH THIS RIGHT NOW...
GOOD IDEA.
I'M GOING TO TRY OUT THAT MOTORCYCLE RACE.
'KAY.
BOOM
BAM
BAM!
POW!
K.O!
TRY AGAIN?
BAM
SIGH.

PFFT. I'VE SEEN TINIER HUMANS DO BETTER.
!
JUST IGNORE IT.
KA-BOOM!
DUN DUN DUN
TRY AGAIN?
SO SOON? HAHA! YOU REALLY SUCK AT THIS.

MISSION FAILED!
TRY AGAIN?
YOU MIGHT ACTUALLY BE THE WORST PLAYER HERE.
HA HA HA!
YOU'RE SO PATHETIC!
GAME OVER!
THAT'S IT!
I'M GONNA CRUSH YOU AND STUFF YOU BACK INTO THE HOLE YOU CAME FROM!
IMPOSSIBLE!
FWIP
HOW CAN A HUMAN LIKE YOU GET A HOLD OF ME?!

WHOOOSH
ARCADE
OH NO YOU DON'T!
YOU'RE LUCKY I'M NOT ZAPPING YOU INTO DUST RIGHT NOW!
SQUEEEZE
NOW WHERE IS THAT STUPID LEAK YOU CRAWLED OUT FROM...?
!
DING♪~
OH HEY, IT'S THAT GUY.
SMACK

TOLD YOU THIS GUY ISN'T ALL THAT HE'S CRACKED UP TO BE.
HAHA, NERD.
!
GRAB
CHOMP
OW, SON OF A—
HEY! BREAK IT UP, YOU TWO!
THIS ISN'T OVER!
DAMN KIDS.
MAX!
THERE YOU ARE. WHAT HAPPENED?

IT WAS ONE OF THOSE BUG THINGS AGAIN.
?
WAS THAT PYPER JUST NOW?
YEAH. I GUESS SHE'S REALLY LEAVING US ALONE NOW.
ANYWAYS, C'MON, LET'S GET OUT OF HERE.
WANNA GRAB SOMETHING TO EAT BEFORE YOU GO BACK HOME?
I DUNNO, I'M NOT REALLY CRAVING ANYTHING.
WAIT, HANG ON...
NOT SO TOUGH NOW, PUNK!
YOU'RE MAKING IT WORSE!

THUD
WHAT THE HELL?
WH-WHAT IS THAT?!
OH, NOW YOU SEE IT?
?
!
AHH! A MONSTER! THERE'S A MONSTER!
WAIT FOR ME!
GOOD LORD. WHAT ARE THOSE KIDS ON ABOUT?
PROBABLY JUST BEING HOODLUMS.
I'LL BE RIGHT BACK. I THINK I FORGOT SOMETHING AT THE MALL.
ALL RIGHT HONEY, I'LL FINISH UP HERE. DON'T BE LONG.

!
MAX! WHAT DID I SAY ABOUT UNNECESSARY TROUBLE?
I DIDN'T NEED YOUR HELP.
I HAD IT UNDER CONTROL!
I WASN'T DOING IT FOR YOU!
BAM
I'M HERE FOR THE MONSTER!
RAHHH!

AHHH!
!
BOOM
DAMN IT!
I WASN'T TRYING TO TRANSFORM!
WHOA! THE OUTFIT IS DIFFERENT! ARE THOSE LEGGINGS?
HEY, THAT'S ALMOST LIKE PANTS!

THAT MEANS IT CAN CHANGE INTO SOMETHING MANLIER, RIGHT?
THAT'S WHAT I THOUGHT, BUT MY MOM SAYS IT'S ALWAYS BEEN DUMB DRESSES.
WELL, THAT MEANS YOU JUST GOTTA BE THE FIRST.
NO WAY...
IS THIS FOR REAL? IS THIS MAGIC? THIS IS UNBELIEVABLE!
IT'S SO CUTE! LOOK AT THOSE SPARKLES!
THE DRESS IS SO SILKY! HOW DOES IT FEEL?
NO! YOU FOOL! YOU'RE SUPPOSED TO BE MISERABLE AND SUPPRESSING YOUR FEELINGS!
STOP IT.
PAP

!
ENOUGH WITH THIS NONSENSE!
NO!
ENOUGH WITH YOU!
BAWOOM
THIS IS JUST THE BEGINNING!
THE FIRST GATE IS ALREADY OPEN—
AHHH!

FIRST GATE?
STAB
THERE WE GO.
POOF
WAY TO GO, MAX!

OH NO. TELL ME SHE DIDN'T SEE ALL THAT.
WHO?
OH MY GOD.
YOU'RE A REAL-LIFE MAGICAL GIRL! JUST LIKE SUNSHINE FROM KAWAII CLOUD!
NO!
I'M A MAGICAL BOY!
ER...I MEAN.
YES, MAX! THAT'S THE SPIRIT! TAKE OWNERSHIP!
MAGICAL BOY?
IS THIS REALLY MY LIFE NOW?

EPISODE 10:
BE A MAN

CHATTER CHATTER
WHISPER
GASP
DO YOU SEE THIS?
I KNOW!
CHATTER
CAN YOU BELIEVE?
CHATTER
CHATTER CHATTER

YOU GOTTA TELL ME MORE ABOUT YOUR ABILITIES.
WHAT ELSE CAN YOU DO? WHERE DID THOSE CREATURES COME FROM?
WHY DO YOU CALL YOURSELF A MAGICAL BOY?
DUDE, CAN YOU NOT? I DON'T WANT ANYTHING TO DO WITH IT.
WHY?
BECAUSE! I JUST WANT TO BE A REGULAR, NON-MAGICAL BOY.
...
BUT WHY?

IT'S JUST HOW I FEEL, OKAY?
I'M NOT A GIRL, I'VE NEVER FELT LIKE ONE, AND THIS WHOLE MAGICAL GIRL THING IS RIDICULOUS.
SO...THAT'S WHY YOU GO BY A MORE MASCULINE NAME LIKE MAX?
SIGH
I STILL DON'T SEE ANYTHING WRONG WITH THE MAGICAL PART.
SURE, YOUR OUTFIT IS FEMININE, BUT GUYS CAN TOTALLY WEAR DRESSES, TOO.
I DON'T SEE YOU WEARING ONE.
EH, I PREFER PANTS. PLUS, WHY NOT MAKE YOUR OUTFIT MORE MASCULINE?
IT'S ALL MAGIC, ISN'T IT?

YOU THINK I HAVEN'T TRIED?!
I CAN'T CONTROL THIS THING! IT'S ALL TIED TO SOME GODDESS'S POWER THAT'S APPARENTLY BEEN THIS WAY FOR CENTURIES.
SNICKER
SNICKER
WHAT ARE YOU LOOKING AT?!
OH SNAP, 'S GONE TO THE DARK SIDE.
HA HA HA

EEP.
GLARE
GASP!
HEY, YOU HAVE TO TEACH ME HOW TO DO THAT.
THE DEATH GLARE.

SORRY IT TOOK ME SO LONG. THE LINE WAS CRAZY, AND PEOPLE ARE ALREADY SPREADING RUMORS THAT YOU'VE BECOME SOME KIND OF DELINQUENT.
CAN YOU BELIEVE IT?
IS THAT WHAT PEOPLE THINK I AM?
I MEAN, PEOPLE HAVE BEEN SAYING YOU GET INTO SOME PRETTY INTENSE FIGHTS...
WELL, IT'S NOT LIKE I GO LOOKING FOR THEM...
TROUBLE FINDS ME, I GUESS.
I MEAN, AS THE OLDEST SON IN MY FAMILY, MY DAD EXPECTS ME TO FOLLOW IN HIS FOOTSTEPS AND UPHOLD HIS REPUTATION OF BEING THE MOST MACHO AND TOUGHEST MAN OUT THERE.
I GUESS THAT'S WHY PEOPLE LIKE TO SEE IF I LIVE UP TO IT.
WHAT DOES YOUR DAD DO? LEAD A MAFIA?

BUT ALL I WANNA DO IS COLLECT CUTE THINGS IN PEACE!
CLANK
CLANK
CLANK
MY ULTIMATE DREAM IS TO BECOME THE PRODUCER OF KAWAII CLOUD'S BEST SUNSHINE GIRL MOVIE!
OF COURSE, MY DAD WOULD KILL ME IF HE EVER FOUND OUT.
BUT THAT WON'T STOP ME.

I'M STILL STUCK WITH THIS STUPID MAGICAL GIRL SITUATION, BECAUSE APPARENTLY THE WORLD WOULD END IF I DON'T DO SOMETHING ABOUT IT.
GOOD FOR YOU.
HEY, BET YOU CAN MAKE IT WORK. HEAR ME OUT.
MAYBE IN ORDER TO MAKE YOUR TRANSFORMATION MORE MASCULINE, YOU, YOURSELF, NEED TO BECOME MANLIER?
AND WHAT BETTER WAY TO LEARN THE ROPES THAN FROM A GUY LIKE ME?
THAT'S RIDICULOUS. MAX IS ALREADY MANLY ENOUGH AS IS.
HMM... MAKES SENSE.

HEY, IF THERE'S A CHANCE I CAN BECOME MANLIER, IMMA TAKE IT.
MY MOM'S BEEN STUFFING "HOW TO BE A LADY" DOWN MY THROAT.
WHAT? YOU CAN'T BE SERIOUS.
IT'S ABOUT TIME I GET A GUY'S PERSPECTIVE ON HOW TO BE A DUDE.
EXACTLY! JUST ONE THING, THOUGH.
PLEASE LET ME FILM YOU IN ACTION WITH ALL YOUR MAGICAL GLORY!
SORRY, WAS THAT KINDA CREEPY?
...IT'S JUST... IT'S JUST NOT EVERY DAY THAT YOU MEET SOME-ONE WITH SUPERPOWERS LIKE SUNSHINE GIRL!
C'MON, MAX, ARE YOU SURE ABOUT THIS? WE BARELY KNOW THIS GUY.
BUT, OF COURSE, YOU'RE NOTHING LIKE HER...SINCE, I MEAN, YOU'RE A DUDE.
IT'S JUST...IT'D BE GREAT MAGIC REFERENCE AND PRACTICE FOR MY FUTURE FILM!

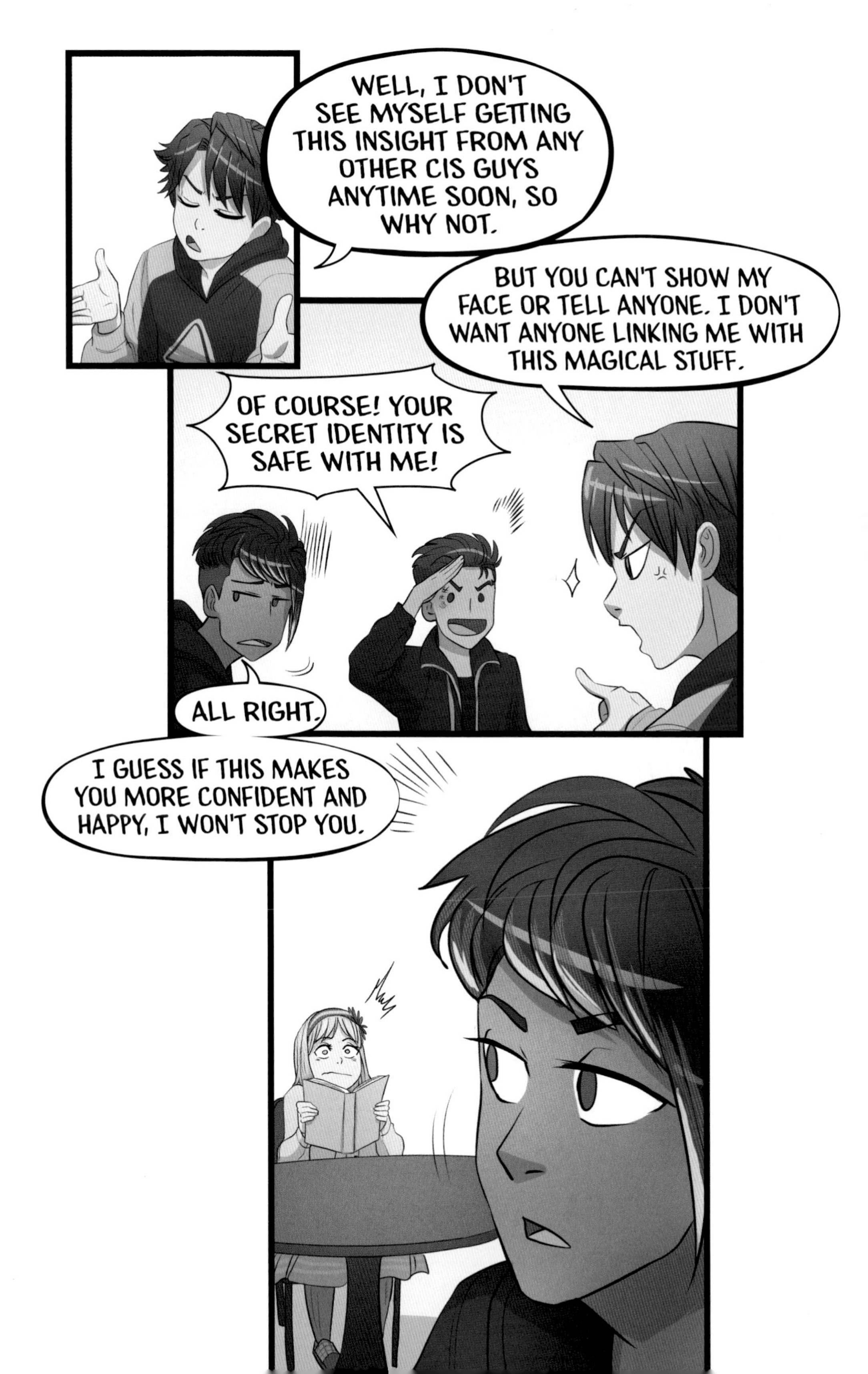
WELL, I DON'T SEE MYSELF GETTING THIS INSIGHT FROM ANY OTHER CIS GUYS ANYTIME SOON, SO WHY NOT.
BUT YOU CAN'T SHOW MY FACE OR TELL ANYONE. I DON'T WANT ANYONE LINKING ME WITH THIS MAGICAL STUFF.
OF COURSE! YOUR SECRET IDENTITY IS SAFE WITH ME!
ALL RIGHT.
I GUESS IF THIS MAKES YOU MORE CONFIDENT AND HAPPY, I WON'T STOP YOU.

UH, I ACTUALLY GOTTA GO CHECK UP ON SOMETHING.
YOU SURE? YOU BARELY TOUCHED YOUR FOOD.
IT'S OKAY. TEXT ME IF YOU NEED ME, 'KAY?
ALL RIGHT, MAX, LET'S BLOW THIS JOINT AND GET STARTED.
WH-WHAT?
THIS IS THE FIRST TIME I'VE SKIPPED CLASS... I DUNNO HOW I FEEL ABOUT THIS.

DON'T WORRY ABOUT IT. SUNSHINE GIRL SKIPS CLASS ALL THE TIME!
THAT... REALLY DOESN'T MAKE ME FEEL ANY BETTER.
NOW, IT'S ALL ABOUT HOW YOU CARRY YOURSELF.
WHEN YOU SIT, YOU'LL WANT TO OPEN UP AND SHOW DOMINANCE.
PLOP
I DUNNO, THAT KINDA LOOKS LIKE AN INVITATION TO GET YOUR BALLS STOMPED ON.
OI, DON'T GET ANY IDEAS. THE POINT IS, IF YOU'RE WOUND UP TIGHT, IT MAKES YOU LOOK TIMID AND SMALL.
UH-HUH.

NOW, WHEN WALKING, PUT SOME SWAG IN YOUR STEP. PLAY WITH IT, AND BE LOOSE.
USE LESS OF YOUR HIPS AND MORE OF YOUR SHOULDERS.
wobble
wobble
wobble
THIS IS MAKING ME OVERLY SELF-CONSCIOUS.
YOU'RE DOING GREAT, JUST DON'T THINK TOO HARD ABOUT IT.

AND WHEN IT COMES TO CONFRONTING PEOPLE,
BE SURE TO MAKE EYE CONTACT.
WHEN YOU NEED TO, DON'T FORGET TO ALWAYS GIVE A FIRM HANDSHAKE. NO FLIMSY HALF-BAKED CRAP.
YOU CAN TELL A LOT ABOUT A MAN FROM THEIR HANDSHAKE.
SIGH.
I DUNNO. ALL OF THIS SEEMS KIND OF...BASIC.
WELL, THAT JUST MEANS YOU'RE A NATURAL. LIKE YOUR FRIEND SAID, YOU'RE ALREADY PLENTY MASCULINE.
I THINK ALL YOU REALLY NEED IS A LITTLE BOOST IN CONFIDENCE.
LIKE CUTTING YOUR HAIR, THESE ARE JUST THINGS THAT MIGHT HELP.

HOW DO YOU FEEL ABOUT THE MEN'S BATHROOM?
AH...I DON'T THINK I'M READY FOR THAT.
WHY NOT?
I MEAN, I DON'T KNOW IF I PASS YET...WHAT IF SOMEONE SEES OR TRIES TO STOP ME?
DON'T WORRY, I'LL STAND GUARD.
PLUS, NO ONE'S GOING TO CARE FOR THE MOST PART.
BUT WHAT IF I NEED TO SIT DOWN TO PEE?
AREN'T PEOPLE GOING TO BE SUSPICIOUS?
JUST GO IN, KEEP TO YOURSELF, DO YOUR BUSINESS, AND GET OUT.
GUYS SIT AND PEE ALL THE TIME.
WE TAKE DUMPS, TOO. SOMETIMES BOTH AT THE SAME TIME.

TROT
TROT
TROT
HUH...
THAT'S A WEIRD-LOOKING CAT.
WALNUT?!
THERE YOU ARE! SHOULDN'T YOU BE AT SCHOOL?
HUFF
HUFF
SHOULDN'T YOU BE AT HOME NAPPING LIKE ALWAYS? WHAT DO YOU WANT?
I'M FINE—
I'VE BEEN SENSING A DISTURBANCE IN THE SEAL LATELY, SO I WAS TRYING TO CHECK UP ON YOU.
AHHHHH!
OH NO, NOW WHAT?

SOMEONE PLEASE HELP! MY BABIES!
THIS IS MUCH FASTER THAN SNEAKING AROUND.
KEKEKE, LOOK AT THEM COWERING IN FEAR!
SO DELICIOUS.
RAHHHH!
BAM!
YOU GUYS ARE GETTING REALLY ANNOYING!
HISS!
WHOOSH

BOOSH
GACK
BAM!
BAM!
BWOOOOM
WHOOSH
AHHH!
MY BABIES! THANK YOU SO MUCH!
I'M SO SORRY, I PROMISE TO BE MORE ATTENTIVE.
WAY TO GO, MA—
MAAAA-GICAL BOY!
THIS IS BAD.
THERE MUST BE A BIGGER LEAK AROUND IF SO MANY MONSTERS OF THIS SIZE ARE APPEARING.

ONE OF THESE PESTS MENTIONED A "GATE" IS OPEN YESTERDAY. DOES THAT MEAN ANYTHING?
IMPOSSIBLE. IT'S TOO SOON FOR THAT...UNLESS YOU HAVEN'T BEEN DOING YOUR JOB.
EXCUSE YOU, THE MONSTER GAVE ME THAT INFORMATION AS I WAS ANNIHILATING IT!
NOW, WHAT'S THIS GATE BUSINESS?
YOU WOULD HAVE ALREADY KNOWN IF YOU'D READ THE BOOK.
WHY WOULD I READ IF YOU COULD JUST TELL ME? YOU'RE SUPPOSED TO BE HELPING ME.
MEOW!
WHAT'S YOUR SIDEKICK SAYING?
HE'S NOT MY SIDEKICK!
HEY! WHERE'RE YOU GOING?!
I NEED TO FOCUS ON FINDING THIS GATE.
FOR NOW, FIND THE LEAK THESE CREATURES ESCAPED FROM JUST NOW.
U-UM.
!

THANK YOU, MA'AM, FOR SAVING US!
MA'AM MA'AM MA'AM MA'AM MA'AM MA'AM
YOU MEAN "SIR"!
THIS IS THE WORK OF THE AMAZING MAGICAL BOY!
MAGICAL BOY?

Episode 11:
CRUSH IT

JEN
You free to come to Bubble Tea House?
Busy atm. So sorry! You ok?
I'm fine! All good.
STUPID CAT WON'T TELL ME SHIT. NOW I GOTTA LOOK THROUGH THIS BRICK.
SIGH...
"LEAKS."
"LEAKS ARE SMALL HOLES CREATED BY LOW-RANKING CREATURES THAT FIND THEIR WAY THROUGH WEAK POINTS WITHIN THE SEAL."
OKAY, I ALREADY KNEW THAT.
"IF MANY LEAKS ARE LEFT UNTREATED, THESE CREATURES WILL GATHER ENOUGH DARK ENERGY TO CREATE A MASSIVE LEAK KNOWN AS A GATE."

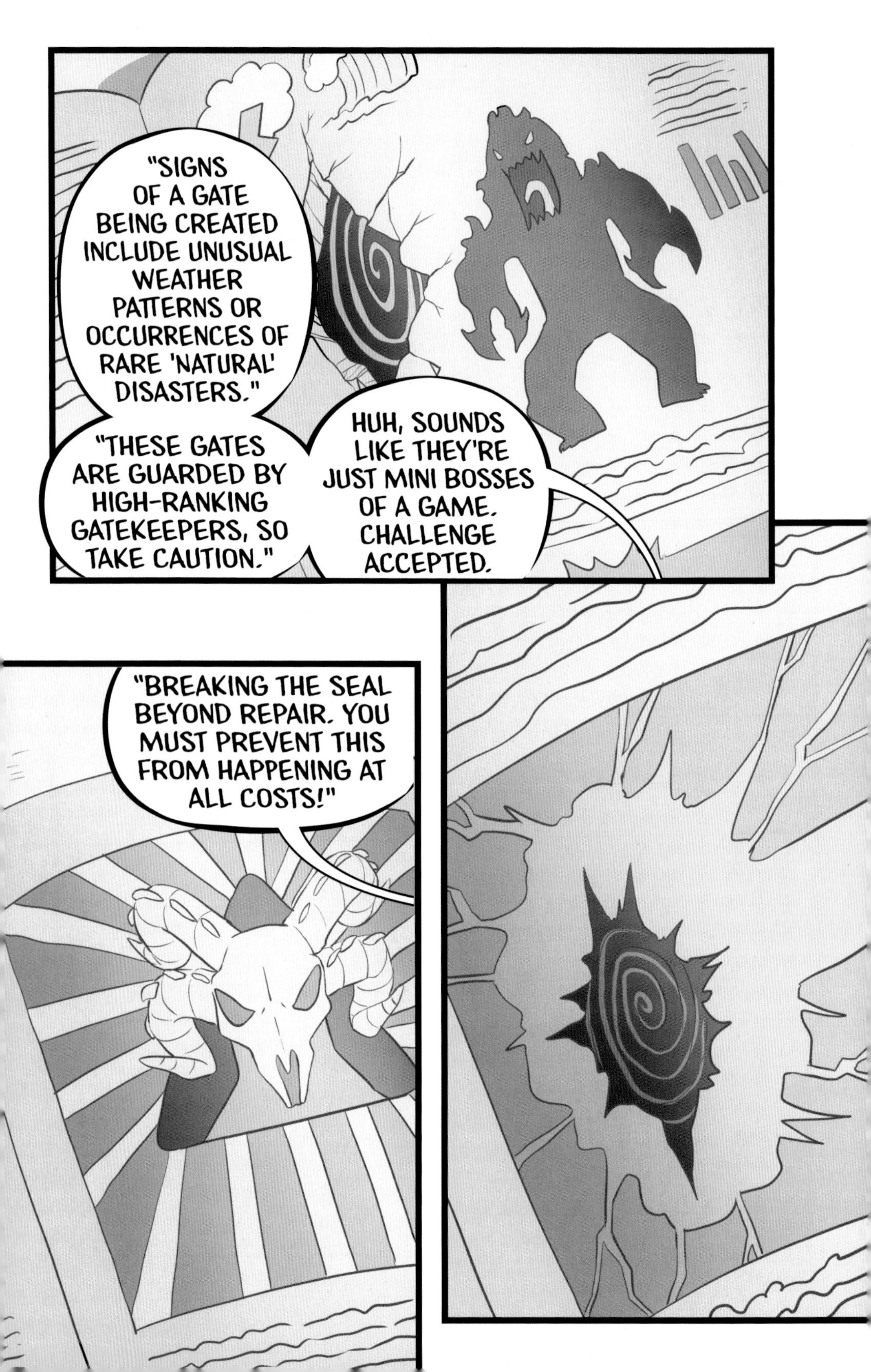
"SIGNS OF A GATE BEING CREATED INCLUDE UNUSUAL WEATHER PATTERNS OR OCCURRENCES OF RARE 'NATURAL' DISASTERS."
"THESE GATES ARE GUARDED BY HIGH-RANKING GATEKEEPERS, SO TAKE CAUTION."
HUH, SOUNDS LIKE THEY'RE JUST MINI BOSSES OF A GAME. CHALLENGE ACCEPTED.
"BREAKING THE SEAL BEYOND REPAIR. YOU MUST PREVENT THIS FROM HAPPENING AT ALL COSTS!"

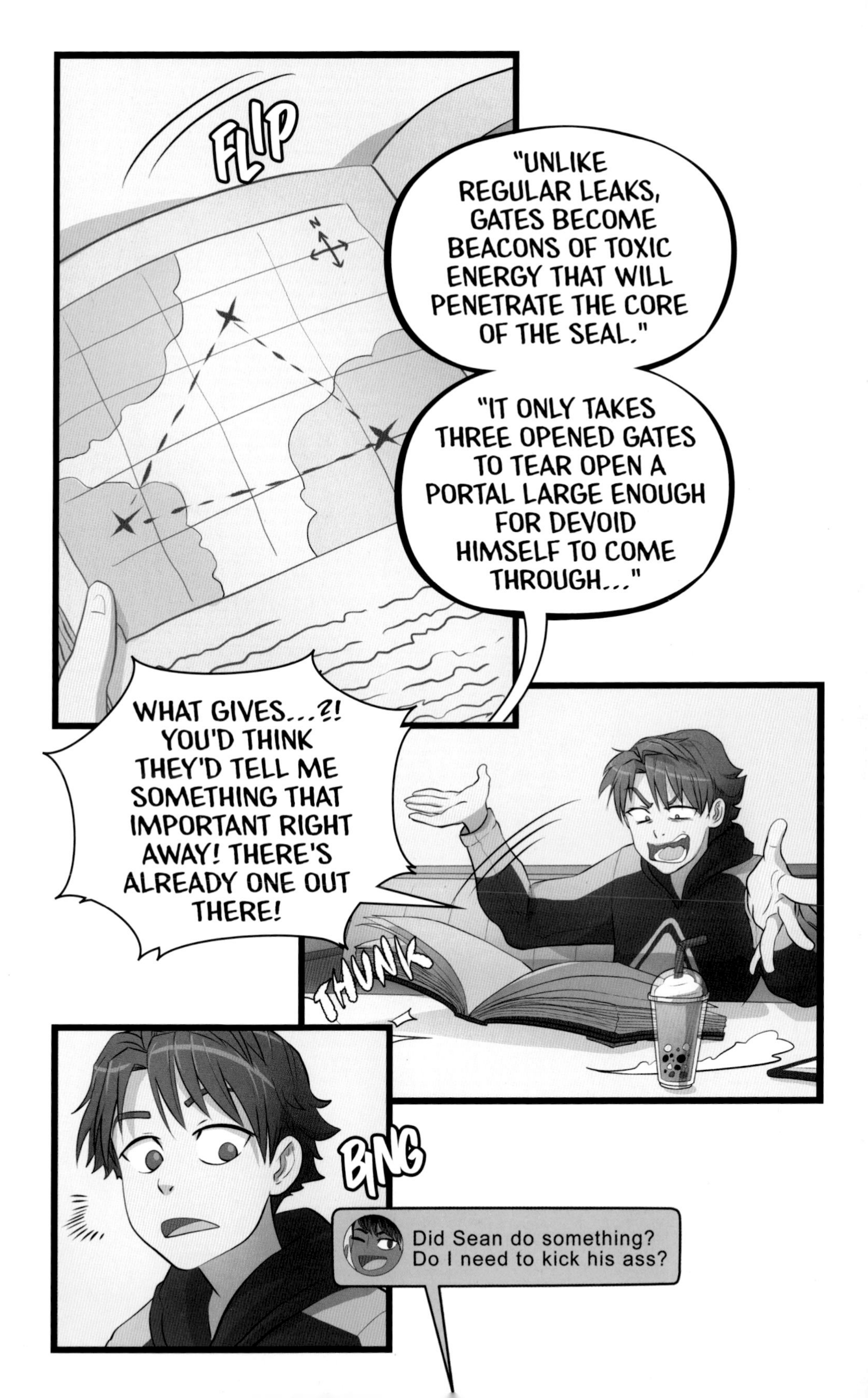
FLIP
"UNLIKE REGULAR LEAKS, GATES BECOME BEACONS OF TOXIC ENERGY THAT WILL PENETRATE THE CORE OF THE SEAL."
"IT ONLY TAKES THREE OPENED GATES TO TEAR OPEN A PORTAL LARGE ENOUGH FOR DEVOID HIMSELF TO COME THROUGH..."
WHAT GIVES...?! YOU'D THINK THEY'D TELL ME SOMETHING THAT IMPORTANT RIGHT AWAY! THERE'S ALREADY ONE OUT THERE!
THUNK
BING
Did Sean do something?
Do I need to kick his ass?

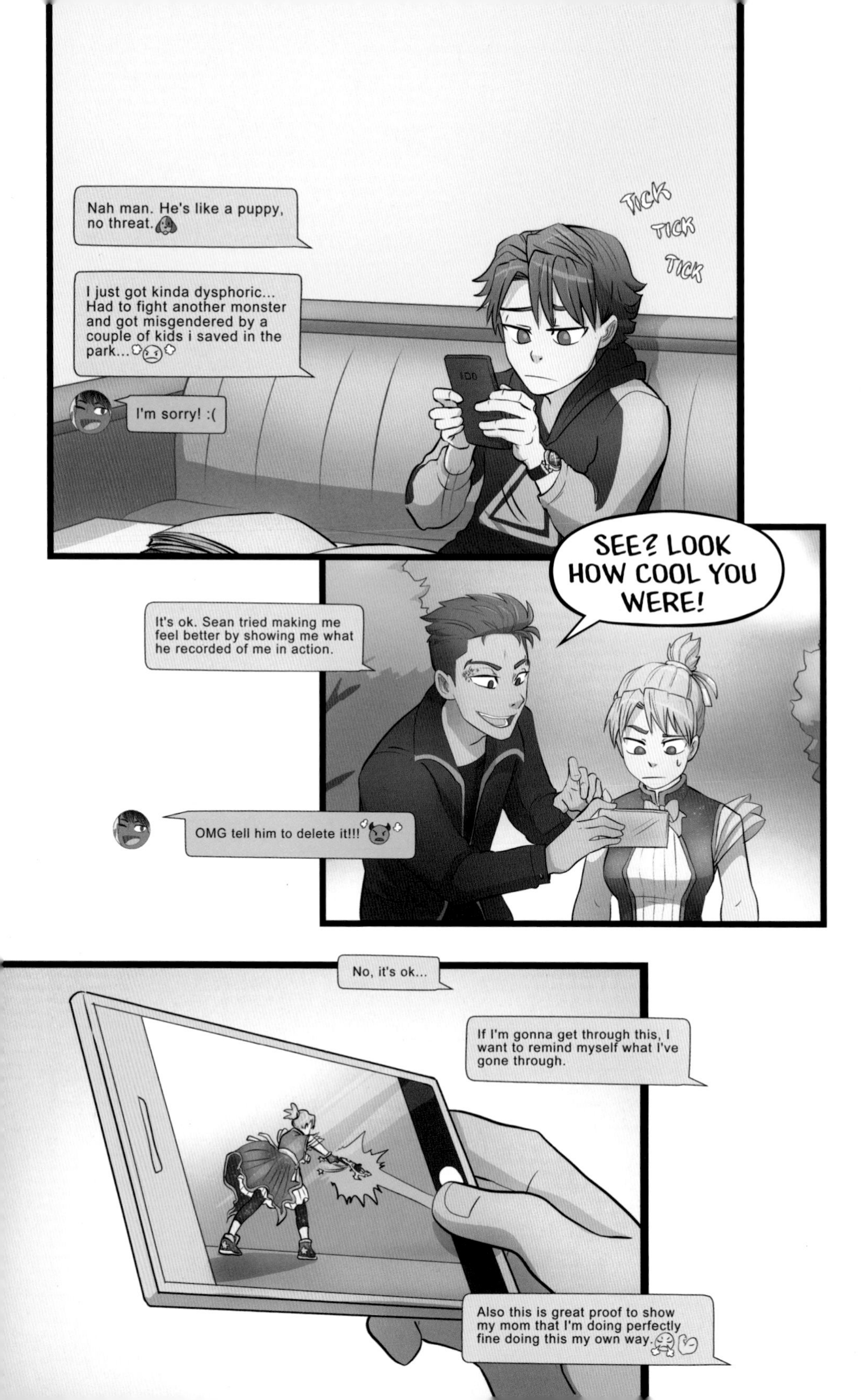
Nah man. He's like a puppy, no threat.
TICK
TICK
TICK
I just got kinda dysphoric... Had to fight another monster and got misgendered by a couple of kids i saved in the park...
I'm sorry! :(
It's ok. Sean tried making me feel better by showing me what he recorded of me in action.
SEE? LOOK HOW COOL YOU WERE!
OMG tell him to delete it!!!
No, it's ok...
If I'm gonna get through this, I want to remind myself what I've gone through.
Also this is great proof to show my mom that I'm doing perfectly fine doing this my own way.

OOoh good point!!
I mean, at least you can barely recognize me in that thing. At least I hope...Plus, I usually just pretend I'm wearing a tight roman robe.
But actually seeing myself in that girly outfit...
kinda killed me inside.

But there was a good thing that happened at least. Check it out!
HE HE HE
YOOOOHHH WHAT ARE THOOOOSSEE?!!!
See, what did I tell you!! You're doing it man. Proud of you.
Right?! There were fewer bows this time too!

IS IT JUST ME, OR HAS PYPER BEEN ACTING SUPER WEIRD LATELY?
TOTALLY, I'VE BEEN GETTING THAT SAME VIBE.
I FEEL LIKE SHE'S IGNORING US.
Crap!!!! Pyper's friends are here!
Quick, escape!!
GIRL, I THINK SHE'S BEEN HANGING OUT WITH YOU-KNOW-WHO.
NO WAY!
YES WAY! I SAW HER WITH MY OWN EYES AFTER LUNCH!
SHUFFLE
SHUFFLE
SHUFFLE
ACK!
DING
Crap Tobi is here!!
Quick, buy him a drink ;D
ARE YOU CRAZY!!
FWOMP
I can't have him see me like this. A loser by himself...
Also I'm trying to escape!

I'LL JUST SNEAK OUT THE BACK.
AH, A STAFF MEMBER! IS THE BACK DOOR OFF-LIMITS?
HAHA, OH HERE'S THE BATHROOM. UH-HUH, YUP.
CREAK
WAIT, I COULD HAVE JUST LEFT. THAT GUY DOESN'T CARE WHAT I DO.
WHY AM I SUCH AN IDIOT?!
SHUT
CRAP!
CLUNK

I'm a fool! I trapped myself in the bathroom. I'm hiding in the men's stalls.
You dork.
ZIP
PSHHHHHH
AHHHHH TOBI'S TAKING A PISS NEAR ME WHAT DO I DO SJKDL;ALSDKFJAJFKDLS
LOL WHAT?
BWOOOM
WHOA!
!
RUMBLE
RUMBLE
REALLY?! ANOTHER EARTH-QUAKE WHILE I'M IN THE BATHROOM?!
AHHHH!
RUMBLE
RUMBLE
CRACK
RUMBLE
CRACK
THIS...ISN'T GOOD.
ZIP
RUMBLE
BOOM
CRACK
RUMBLE
CRACK
KEKEKE NOW IT'S MY TIME TO SHINE!
WHAT THE HECK?!
WHOOOSH

OH NO, PLEASE TELL ME THAT ISN'T A MONSTER...
A M-MONSTER?!
DAMN IT!
WHAT DO I DO?! I CAN'T TRANSFORM IN FRONT OF TOBI! BUT IF I DON'T, HE MIGHT GET HURT!
LOOK AT THESE HUMANS, SUCH EASY PREY!
THE RUMORS OF THE NEXT DESCENDANT OF AURORA INTERFERING MUST BE A JOKE!
WE'VE ALREADY OPENED THE SECOND GATE SO EFFORTLESSLY!
WHO YOU CALLIN' A JOKE?!
MAX?
!
TOBI!
THUD
GET OFF HIM!
THUNK
WH-WHAT'S GOING ON? WHY DO I FEEL SO LIGHT-HEADED?
HOLD ON.

WHOOSH
WHOOSH
WHOA! WHAT THE HECK?
SHOVE
WHO DO YOU THINK YOU ARE?
CRAP! TOBI, ARE YOU OKAY?
OH, COME ON, DID YOU JUST GET BIGGER FROM ABSORBING TOBI'S LIGHT FART?
JEEZ, I THOUGHT THESE CREATURES WANTED TO ABSORB DARK LIGHT, NOT KILL US IMMEDIATELY!
FEAR ME, HUMAN!
WHOOSH
THUNK
THUNK
THUNK
OKAY, HE'S PASSED OUT. IT SHOULD BE SAFE TO TRANSFORM.
BUT WHAT IF HE DOES WAKE UP AND SEES ME?

I WILL NOT BE MADE A FOOL OF ON MY FIRST ARRIVAL!
JUST TRANSFORM.
OOF!
BAM
FRICK!
THUNK
GASP
!
FLIP
KICK
C'MON, TIME TO TRANSFORM NOW!
THUD
WHY ISN'T IT WORKING RIGHT AWAY LIKE LAST TIME?!
!
SMACK
GET AWAY FROM HIM!

AURORA! I'M BEGGING YOU, WORK, DAMMIT!
BWOOSH
BELIEVE, AND IT WILL.
AHHHH!
ZAP
ZAP
ZAP
THIS CAN'T BE!
YOU CAN'T POSSIBLY BE THE DESCENDANT OF AURORA!
WELL, IT IS WHAT IT IS!

IT'S GOING TO BE OKAY, TOBI. YOU'RE OKAY.
A-AM...I DREAMING?
TOBI!
IS ANYONE IN HERE? ARE YOU ALL RIGHT?
CREAK
...
THIS... ISN'T WHAT YOU THINK.
I...I'M NOT SURE WHAT TO THINK.
FANTASTIC! SHOULD REALLY CHECK ON THAT GUY, THOUGH, 'KAY?
THANKS, BYE!
? ? ?

Episode 12: CONFRONTATION

CHATTER
TAP
TAP
TAP
CHATTER
CHATTER
TOBI!
TOBI, WAIT UP!
HEY, I'M TALKING TO YOU!
PAT
OH, HEY, !
JUST THE GIRL I WAS LOOKING FOR.
?!
DID HE JUST...?
MAYBE I DIDN'T HEAR HIM RIGHT.
A-ARE YOU OKAY, TOBI?
OF COURSE! YOU'RE THE MAGICAL GIRL WHO SAVED ME.
WHY DON'T YOU TAKE PRIDE IN YOUR FEMININITY MORE OFTEN AND HONOR YOUR REAL NAME, ?

YOU WERE SO BEAUTIFUL. IT'D BE SUCH A WASTE TO HIDE IT.
NO NO NO
I THINK YOU SHOULD WEAR A DRESS MORE OFTEN.
NO NO
WHAT ARE YOU SAYING, TOBI?
THIS CAN'T BE HAPPENING.
THUNK
NOW HE REALLY DOESN'T SEE ME AS A MAN.
AM I EVEN MAN ENOUGH? WHO AM I TRYING TO FOOL?

WHAT IF...
WHAT IF HE'S
RIGHT...
WHOOSH
Have
faith.
WAIT A
MINUTE.
WHO YOU
CALLING A
WASTE?!
SMACK
I'M HOT
AS A MAN!

REOW!
THUD
AH...
IT WAS A NIGHTMARE.
HOW DARE IT USE TOBI!
THAT WAS COMPLETELY...
GASP
UNCALLED FOR!
HEY, NOT MY FAULT YOU WERE ALL UP IN MY SPACE. I WAS ASLEEP.
BESIDES, YOU'RE A CAT! SHOULDN'T YOU HAVE BETTER REFLEXES?

YOU'RE LOSING YOUR TOUCH...
MR. "I CAN SENSE LEAKS BUT COMPLETELY MISS TWO GATES."
HOW DARE YOU! IT'S NEVER GOTTEN THIS BAD WITH PREVIOUS GODDESSES!
YOU'RE...
SQUISH
SQUISH
WHAT'RE YOU TRYIN' TO SAY, HUH?
CLEARLY NOT LIKE THE OTHER GODDESSES.
EXACTLY!
I WOULDN'T CONSIDER THAT A GOOD THING!
IT'S TAKEN YOU LONGER TO SHOW SIGNS OF YOUR POWERS, AND YOUR UNORTHODOX WAYS OF DEVELOPING YOUR SKILLS HAVE BEEN QUESTIONABLE.
IT'S UNUSUAL AND I DO NOT UNDERSTAND IT!
THAT DOESN'T MEAN MY WAY IS WORSE.
MAYBE NOT.
BUT YOU'RE NOT TAKING YOUR RESPONSIBILITY SERIOUSLY ENOUGH LIKE YOUR PREDECESSORS DID.

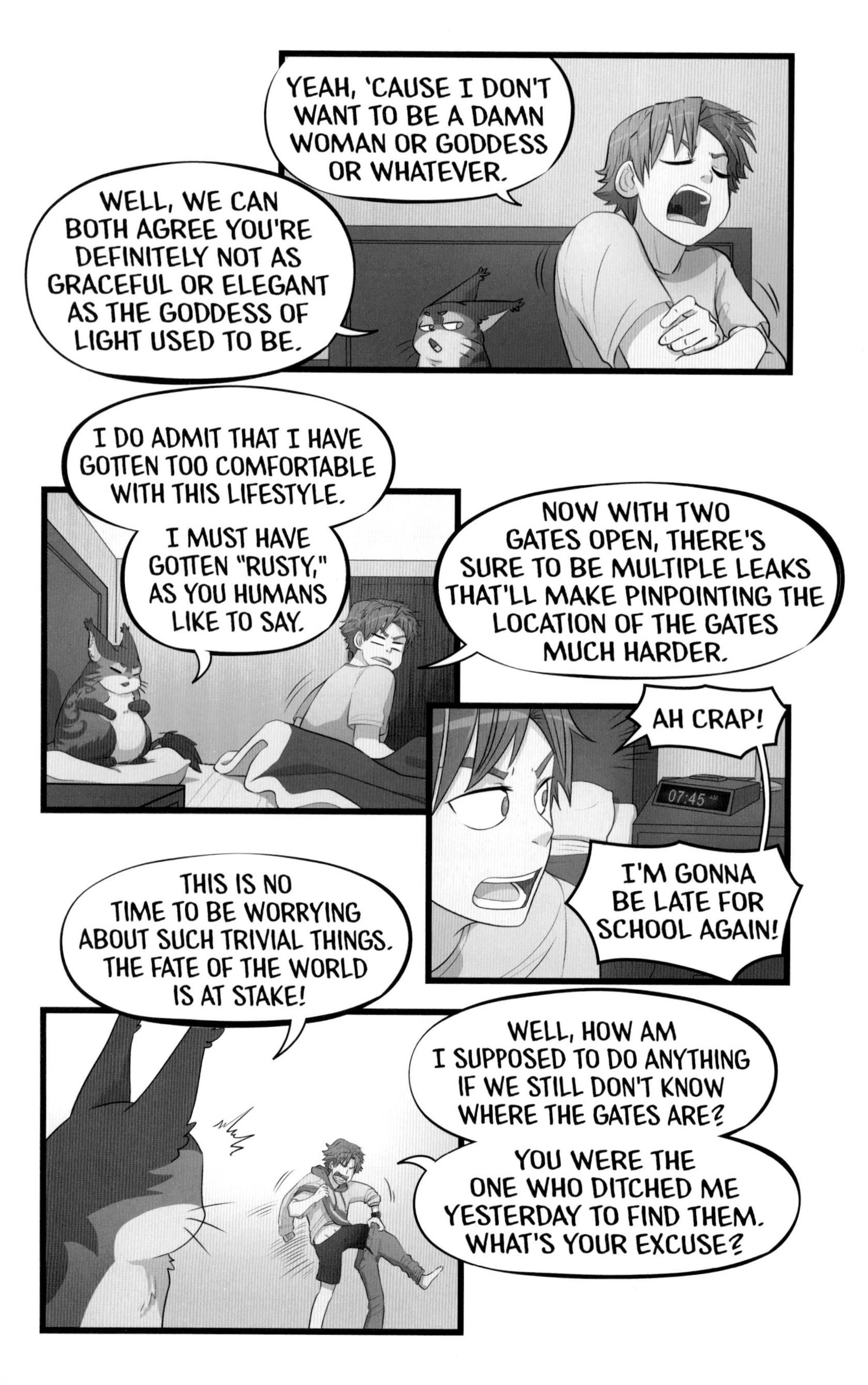
YEAH, 'CAUSE I DON'T WANT TO BE A DAMN WOMAN OR GODDESS OR WHATEVER.
WELL, WE CAN BOTH AGREE YOU'RE DEFINITELY NOT AS GRACEFUL OR ELEGANT AS THE GODDESS OF LIGHT USED TO BE.
I DO ADMIT THAT I HAVE GOTTEN TOO COMFORTABLE WITH THIS LIFESTYLE.
I MUST HAVE GOTTEN "RUSTY," AS YOU HUMANS LIKE TO SAY.
NOW WITH TWO GATES OPEN, THERE'S SURE TO BE MULTIPLE LEAKS THAT'LL MAKE PINPOINTING THE LOCATION OF THE GATES MUCH HARDER.
AH CRAP!
07:45 AM
I'M GONNA BE LATE FOR SCHOOL AGAIN!
THIS IS NO TIME TO BE WORRYING ABOUT SUCH TRIVIAL THINGS. THE FATE OF THE WORLD IS AT STAKE!
WELL, HOW AM I SUPPOSED TO DO ANYTHING IF WE STILL DON'T KNOW WHERE THE GATES ARE?
YOU WERE THE ONE WHO DITCHED ME YESTERDAY TO FIND THEM. WHAT'S YOUR EXCUSE?

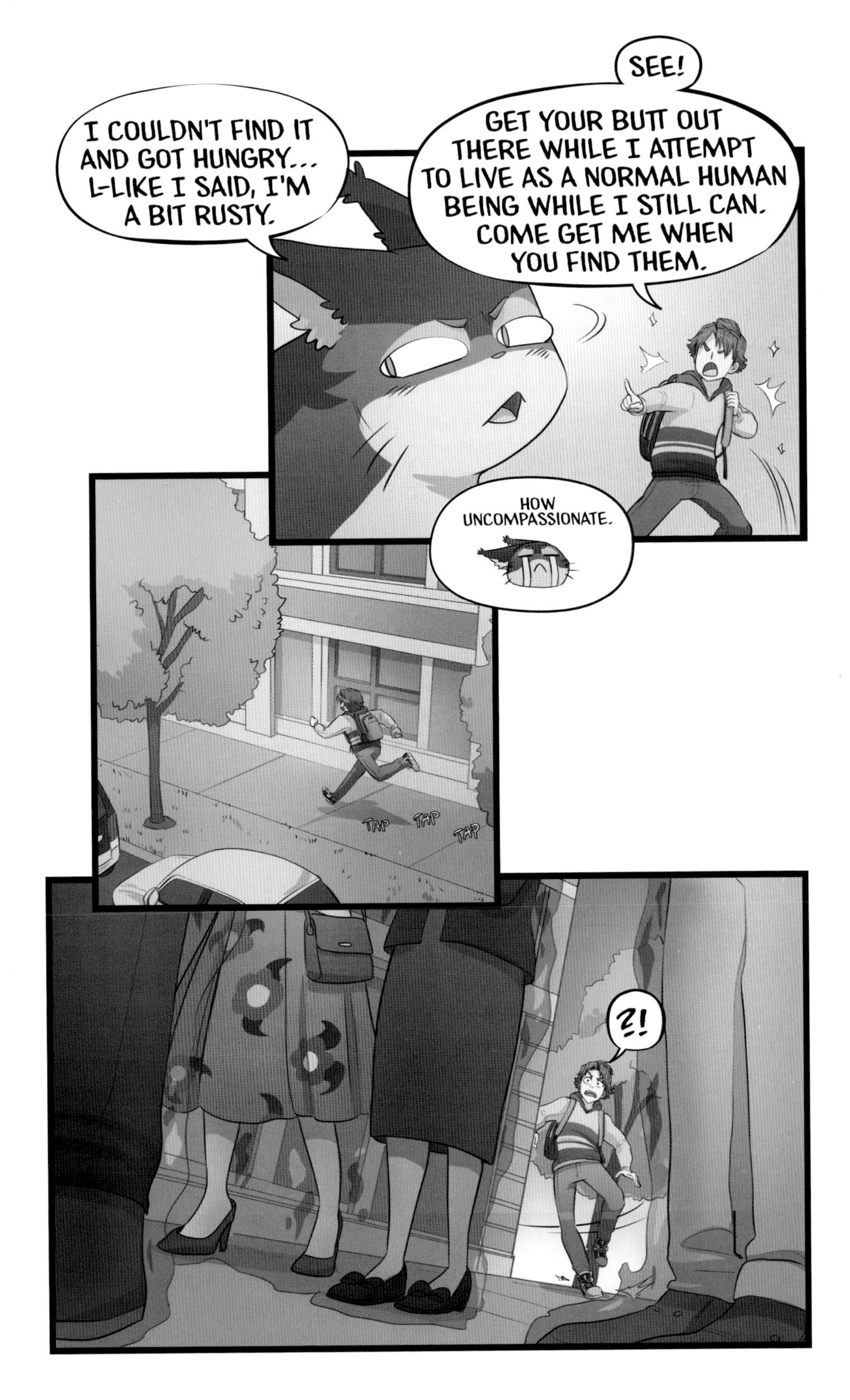

I COULDN'T FIND IT AND GOT HUNGRY... L-LIKE I SAID, I'M A BIT RUSTY.
SEE!
GET YOUR BUTT OUT THERE WHILE I ATTEMPT TO LIVE AS A NORMAL HUMAN BEING WHILE I STILL CAN. COME GET ME WHEN YOU FIND THEM.
HOW UNCOMPASSIONATE.
TAP
TAP
TAP
?!

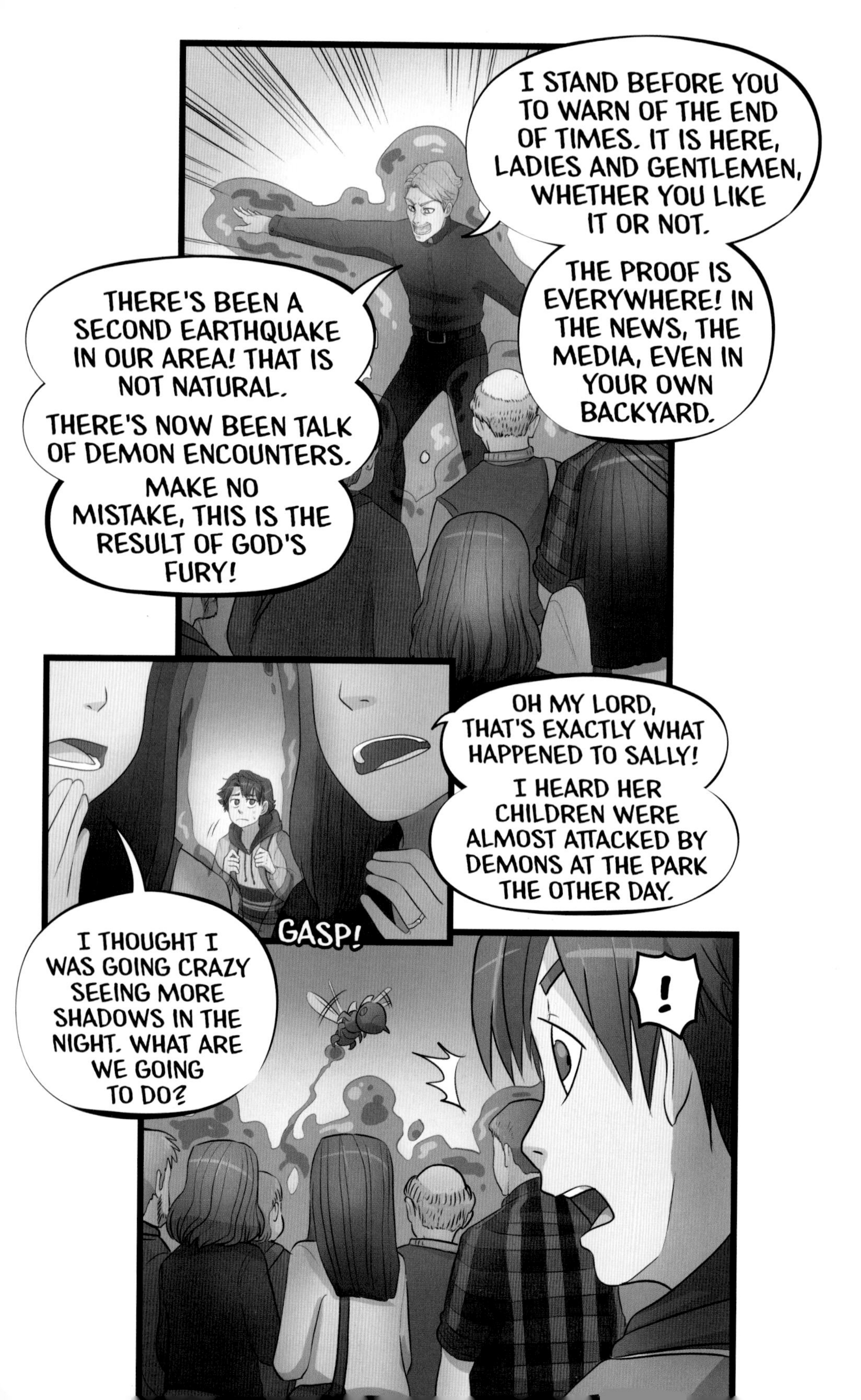
I STAND BEFORE YOU TO WARN OF THE END OF TIMES. IT IS HERE, LADIES AND GENTLEMEN, WHETHER YOU LIKE IT OR NOT.
THE PROOF IS EVERYWHERE! IN THE NEWS, THE MEDIA, EVEN IN YOUR OWN BACKYARD.
THERE'S BEEN A SECOND EARTHQUAKE IN OUR AREA! THAT IS NOT NATURAL.
THERE'S NOW BEEN TALK OF DEMON ENCOUNTERS.
MAKE NO MISTAKE, THIS IS THE RESULT OF GOD'S FURY!
OH MY LORD, THAT'S EXACTLY WHAT HAPPENED TO SALLY!
I HEARD HER CHILDREN WERE ALMOST ATTACKED BY DEMONS AT THE PARK THE OTHER DAY.
GASP!
I THOUGHT I WAS GOING CRAZY SEEING MORE SHADOWS IN THE NIGHT. WHAT ARE WE GOING TO DO?
!

HEY, STOP THAT!
WHOOOSH
DID SHE JUST TRY TO SILENCE PASTOR RYLAND?
THIS IS WHY THE WORLD IS IN SHAMBLES NOW.
KIDS THESE DAYS DON'T HAVE MANNERS, RUNNING THEIR MOUTHS LIKE THAT.

BZZZZZZ
UGH, STUPID MONSTERS. THEY NEED TO DISAPPEAR!
YOU!
I'D KNOW THAT LIGHT ANYWHERE!
GASP
SHOW ME WHERE THE FREAKIN' GATE IS OR I'LL BLAST YOU INTO BITS!
I'LL NEVER TELL YOU!

BOOOSH
!
WAIT, DID YOU SEE THAT?
C'MON, WE'RE GOING TO BE LATE.
BUT...
LOOK, IT'S THE MAGICAL GIRL FROM LAST TIME!
YOU MEAN MAGICAL BOY.
HUFF
WHOOSH
I MADE IT HERE ON TIME.
HUFF
HUFF
HUFF
HUFF
HUFF
OH SH—
NOW IF ONLY I COULD CHANGE BACK...
YO, DID YOU FEEL THE EARTHQUAKE LAST NIGHT?
YEAH, AT FIRST I THOUGHT IT WAS A TRUCK DRIVING BY, BUT BOY, WAS I WRONG.
DANG IT, LEMME CHANGE BACK ALREADY!
MAX?
AH.
POOF

YOU GOOD?
Y-YEAH.
IT'S BEEN A WILD MORNING.
OH NO, NOT THEM AGAIN!
OMG, I JUST SAW PYPER WITH THAT DEGENERATE AGAIN. I KNEW SOMETHING WAS OFF EVER SINCE SHE STOPPED SHOWING UP FOR CHOIR PRACTICE.
AND HERE I THOUGHT IT WAS JUST BECAUSE SHE WASN'T FEELING WELL.
SEAN!
SHE'S PROBABLY SECRETLY GAY HERSELF.
MAYBE THAT'S WHAT CAUSED THE EARTHQUAKE.
YEAH, FEELING SICK, MY BUTT. PEOPLE ARE ALWAYS PUTTING HER UP ON A PEDESTAL BECAUSE HER DAD'S THE PASTOR.
HEH
YOU KNOW YOU SHOULDN'T TALK BEHIND PEOPLE'S BACKS LIKE THAT.
AHH!
GET AWAY, YOU PERVERT!
THEY SURE HAVE BEEN TALKING A LOT OF TRASH ABOUT PYPER. I KINDA FEEL BAD FOR HER.

OH, HEY, THERE'S JEN.
HEY, JEN, WAIT UP!
WHOOSH
YO! JEN!
HEY!
AH...

Episode 13:

TEAM MAGICAL BOY

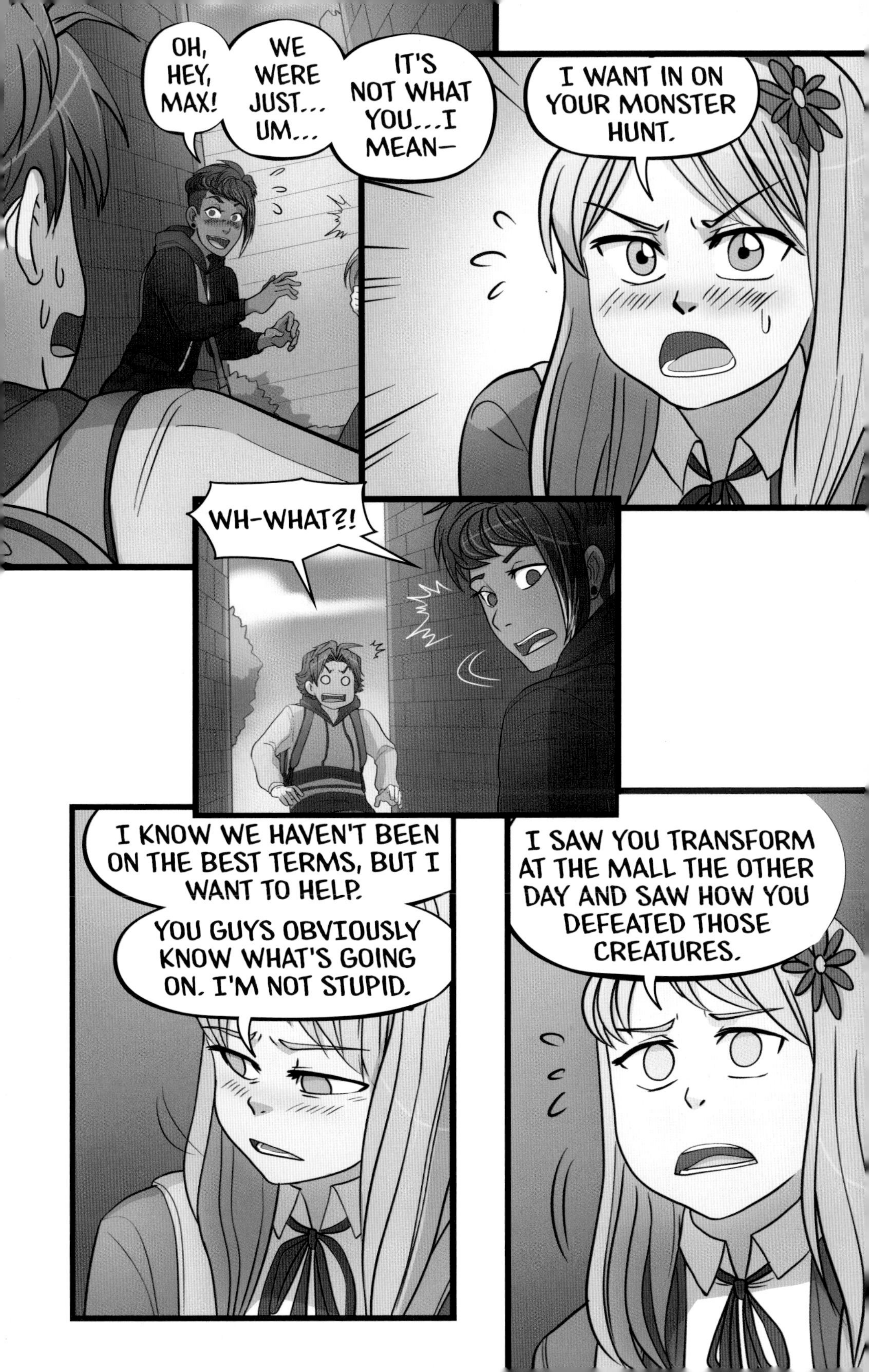
OH, HEY, MAX!
WE WERE JUST... UM...
IT'S NOT WHAT YOU...I MEAN—
I WANT IN ON YOUR MONSTER HUNT.
WH-WHAT?!
I KNOW WE HAVEN'T BEEN ON THE BEST TERMS, BUT I WANT TO HELP.
YOU GUYS OBVIOUSLY KNOW WHAT'S GOING ON. I'M NOT STUPID.
I SAW YOU TRANSFORM AT THE MALL THE OTHER DAY AND SAW HOW YOU DEFEATED THOSE CREATURES.

I'VE ONLY JUST BEGUN ACCEPTING MYSELF FOR WHO I AM, BUT I'M TIRED OF MY DAD BLAMING ALL THESE EARTHQUAKES AND MONSTERS ON SINNERS.
IT'S NOT RIGHT. I NEED TO PROVE HIM...TO PROVE TO MYSELF...THAT HE'S WRONG.
SO PLEASE...
PLEASE, GIVE ME A CHANCE TO HELP.
WHOA, THERE'S A WHOLE PARTY OVER HERE.
IS HE IN ON THIS, TOO?
IN ON WHAT? TEAM MAGICAL BOY? HECK, YEAH, I AM!

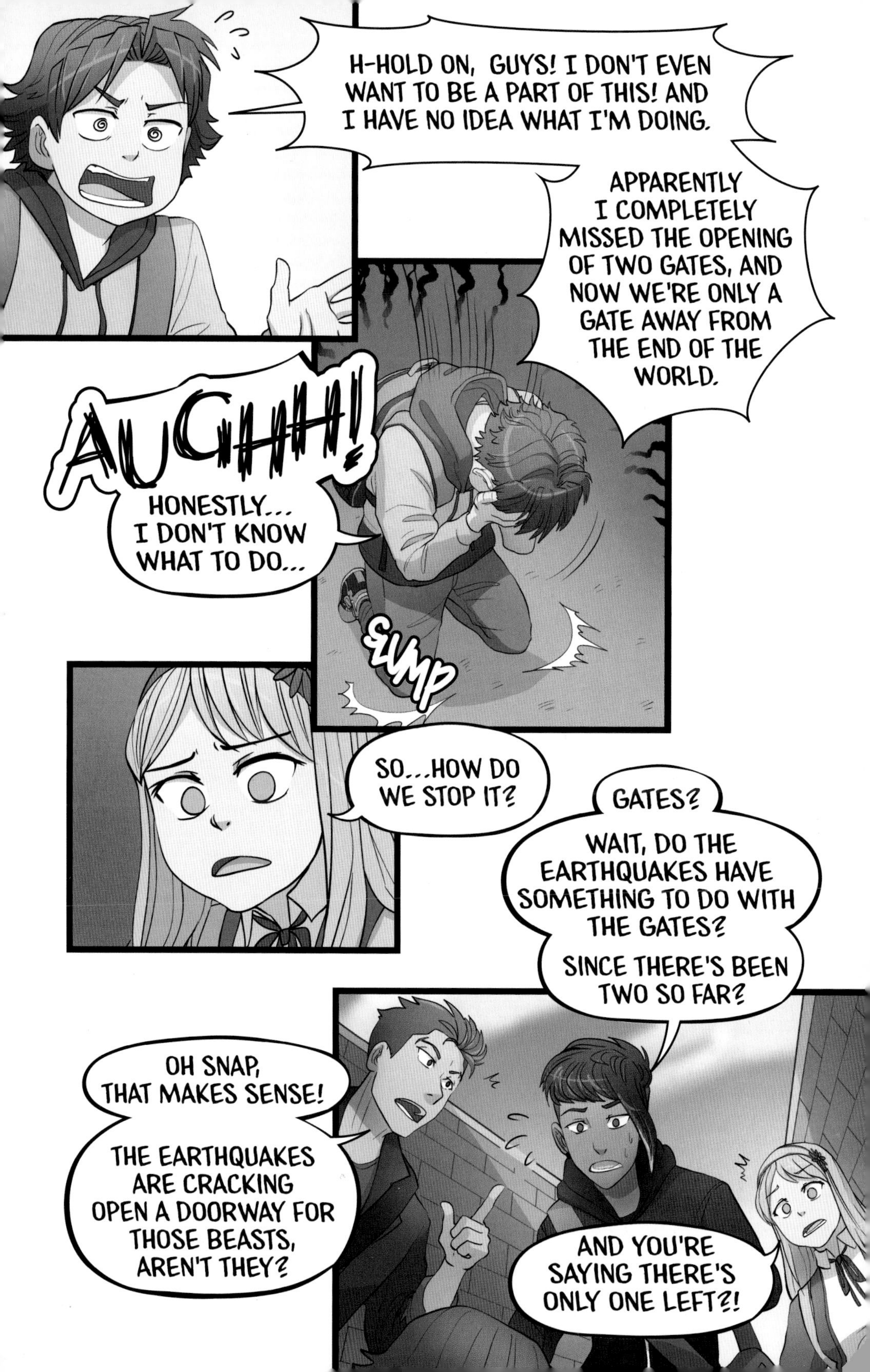
H-HOLD ON, GUYS! I DON'T EVEN WANT TO BE A PART OF THIS! AND I HAVE NO IDEA WHAT I'M DOING.
APPARENTLY I COMPLETELY MISSED THE OPENING OF TWO GATES, AND NOW WE'RE ONLY A GATE AWAY FROM THE END OF THE WORLD.
AUGHH!
HONESTLY... I DON'T KNOW WHAT TO DO...
SLUMP
SO...HOW DO WE STOP IT?
GATES?
WAIT, DO THE EARTHQUAKES HAVE SOMETHING TO DO WITH THE GATES?
SINCE THERE'S BEEN TWO SO FAR?
OH SNAP, THAT MAKES SENSE!
THE EARTHQUAKES ARE CRACKING OPEN A DOORWAY FOR THOSE BEASTS, AREN'T THEY?
AND YOU'RE SAYING THERE'S ONLY ONE LEFT?!

WE?!
NO
NO
NO
THERE'S NO "WE."
C'MON, MAX, LET HER HELP.
SERIOUSLY. I KNOW THIS IS KINDA WEIRD AND SUDDEN BUT...
I CAN EXPLAIN LATER. WE CAN TRUST PYPER, I PROMISE.
IT'S NOT ABOUT THAT. I WAS BARELY ABLE TO KEEP TOBI SAFE LAST NIGHT WHEN THE EARTHQUAKE HIT.
OH RIGHT, YOU RAN INTO HIM AT BUBBLE TEA HOUSE...
WAIT! DID HE SEE YOU TRANSFORM AND EVERYTHING?

MAYBE? I DUNNO. HE WAS PASSED OUT, I THINK.
BUT THE FACT IS...
I HAD TROUBLE TRANSFORMING, AND THESE MONSTERS ARE ONLY GETTING MORE AGGRESSIVE. I DON'T KNOW WHAT I'D DO IF ANY-THING HAPPENED TO YOU... OR ANY OF YOU GUYS!
AND BESIDES, GIVE ME SOME CREDIT. I CAN HANDLE MYSELF.
HEY, THE MORE REASON YOU SHOULDN'T BE DOING THIS ALONE.
YEAH, BRING IT ON.
I OWE THEM SOME PAYBACK FOR WHAT THEY DID TO ME AT THE MALL.
AND I'M DEFINITELY NOT GOING TO LET THEM PREY ON ME AGAIN WITHOUT A FIGHT.
PAT

EVEN SO, I DON'T EVEN KNOW WHERE THE GATES ARE.
WALNUT ISN'T BEING HELPFUL AT ALL.
WALNUT?
HIS ANIMAL SIDEKICK.
HE'S NOT MY SIDEKICK! JUST A USELESS FAT CAT.
OKAY...
WHAT **DO** YOU KNOW ABOUT THE GATES?
WELL... JUST THAT IT TAKES THREE TO UNLEASH THE KING OF DARKNESS, DEVOID.
AND WHAT'S THIS INTERFERENCE YOUR CAT MENTIONED?

I DUNNO, MAN. WHEN A GATE IS OPENED, IT WEAKENS THE SEAL, WHICH TRIGGERS MORE LEAKS TO OPEN AROUND IT.
I'M GUESSING THE CLUTTER IS MESSING WITH HIS SENSES.
THAT'S IT, THEN! THE MORE LEAKS, THE MORE MONSTERS, RIGHT? WE CAN MAP OUT WHERE THEY'RE APPEARING MOST AND MAYBE PINPOINT THE GATE THAT WAY?
HECK YEAH, LET'S DO THIS!
THE SOONER WE FIND THESE GATES, THE SOONER YOU CAN PATCH THEM UP AND BE A MAN.
FWIP
WHAT THE HECK, SEAN!! PUT THAT AWAY!
WE CAN'T RUN AROUND WITH KNIVES LIKE LUNATICS IN BROAD DAYLIGHT! WE'RE GONNA GET ARRESTED BEFORE WE CAN DO ANYTHING!
PLUS, I HAVE NO IDEA IF A KNIFE WOULD EVEN WORK AGAINST THOSE BUGS.
WON'T KNOW TILL YOU TRY.

MAX IS RIGHT. LET'S HEAD TO CLASS FOR NOW AND MEET UP LATER TONIGHT TO COME UP WITH A PLAN.
YEAH! TEAM MAGICAL BOY MOVE OUT!
RING
RING
RING
RING
H-HEY! DID YOU GUYS NOT HEAR ME—
OKAY...I MEAN, I'M NOT COMPLETELY SOLD, BUT I TRUST YOU.
SO ARE YOU GONNA EXPLAIN **THAT**, OR WHAT?
I WAS GONNA TELL YOU, I SWEAR! IT'S JUST...

WELL, A LOT HAS HAPPENED SINCE THAT NIGHT WE SAVED HER.
I WANTED TO KEEP A CLOSE EYE ON HER TO MAKE SURE SHE WAS OKAY. TURNS OUT WHAT WE SAID REALLY STUCK WITH HER.
CHATTER
CHATTER
TICK
TICK
CHATTER
CHATTER
CHATTER
CHATTER
YO, SO I'VE BEEN GIVING THIS SOME THOUGHT.
SLAP

SKIT
SCRCH
SCR
I STARTED MAPPING OUT THE PLACES WHERE WE'VE ALREADY ENCOUNTERED MONSTERS.
FOR EXAMPLE, BUBBLE TEA HOUSE HAS BEEN A HOT SPOT FOR TWO KNOWN ATTACKS.
THEN THERE WAS THAT ONE IN THE MALL THAT ATTACKED ME, AND THAT ONE TIME WITH KIDS AT THE PARK NEAR THE SCHOOL.
RIGHT.
SIGH
YOU GUYS REALLY AREN'T GOING TO LET ME DO THIS ALONE, ARE YOU?
NOPE.
IN THAT CASE... THE FIRST ONE I RAN INTO DIDN'T COME FROM BUBBLE TEA HOUSE.
I RAN INTO IT ON MY WAY THERE.
AND WHERE WAS THAT?
IT WAS MORE TOWARD HERE, AND I FOUND THE LEAK IT CAME FROM IN THIS ALLEYWAY...
NEAR HERE.
THAT'S NEAR THE PARK.
SCRITCH
SCRIT
AND THE MALL ISN'T TOO FAR FROM THERE, EITHER.

SO, THE PLAN IS TO MEET UP AT THE PARK AFTER DARK?
I THINK THAT'D BE A GOOD START.
OMG, ARE YOU SERIOUS, PYPER?
WHAT'S YOUR FATHER GOING TO SAY IF HE SEES YOU HANGING OUT WITH THESE DEGENERATES?
WELL, IF I REMEMBER CORRECTLY, "THOU SHALT LOVE THY NEIGHBOR AS THYSELF." I'M NOT DOING ANYTHING WRONG.
WOW, HYPOCRITE MUCH?
YOU WERE THE ONE THAT WAS BAD-MOUTHING THEM FIRST.
I-I WAS IN A BAD PLACE, AND I'M LEARNING TO BE BETTER.
SO...PLEASE FORGIVE ME.
WOW, REALLY? YOU'RE JUST GOING TO START ACTING ALL HIGH-AND-MIGHTY NOW AND MAKE US LOOK BAD?
WE'RE DONE. YOU'RE TOTALLY DEAD TO US.
PYPER...

FINALLY! YOU'RE SO MUCH BETTER OFF WITHOUT THEM!
A-AND DON'T WORRY, WE'RE COOL NOW.
THANKS... MAX, RIGHT?
AWW, THIS IS ADORABLE.
SHUT UP.
AAALL RIGHT, GUYS, I GUESS I'LL SEE YOU ALL AT THE PARK AROUND 6:00, Y-YEAH?
SURE THING.
WHERE YOU GOIN'?

...
WHERE'S MAX GOING?
OH, HEY, TOBI, WHAT'S UP?
AH, I JUST HAD A QUESTION FOR MAX, BUT I GUESS I'LL CATCH 'EM ANOTHER TIME.
I'LL SEE YOU GUYS AROUND.
ISN'T THAT THE GUY MAX SAVED LAST NIGHT?
YEAH.
ARE WE NOT GOING TO TELL HIM?
BEST NOT. WE DON'T KNOW FOR SURE WHAT HE KNOWS.
AND I'M PRETTY SURE MAX WOULDN'T WANT TO GET HIM INVOLVED.
HMM.
SO... HOW EXACTLY ARE WE GOING TO HELP MAX AGAINST THESE MONSTERS?

Episode 14:

WALK IN THE PARK

IS EVERYONE HERE?
PRESENT AND READY TO ROLL.
WHERE'S MAX?
I'M HERE.
YOU BROUGHT YOUR CAT?
HE INSISTED ON COMING, BUT GOT TIRED HALFWAY.
LAZY BUTT.
SO WHAT ARE WE GOING TO DO, EXACTLY?
TROT
WELL, BASED ON THE MAP, THIS SHOULD BE ONE OF THE HOTSPOTS FOR THOSE MONSTERS.
TROT
TROT

I RECKON ONE WILL SHOW UP SOON, AND WE'LL JUST FOLLOW IT.
THAT'S NOT MUCH OF A PLAN AT ALL.
YEAH, AND YOU GUYS WON'T BE ABLE TO SEE ANY OF THEM UNLESS THEY'RE LIKE... BIG ENOUGH.
SKIT
SKIT
SKIT
YOU MEAN LIKE THAT?
QUICK, FOLLOW IT!
TSK
TSK
TSK
SHOOT, I DIDN'T SEE WHAT WAY IT WENT.
ARE YOU SURE YOU SAW A MONSTER AND NOT JUST SOME SQUIRREL?
I'LL HAVE YOU KNOW I HAVE A KEEN EYE FOR DETAILS! I KNOW WHAT I SAW.
EVEN IF WE DO FIND IT AND THE GATE, HOW ARE YOU GUYS GOING TO HELP?
WITH EMOTIONAL SUPPORT!
PLUS, IF THERE'S A SWARM, WE GOT YOUR BACK.

I MEAN, OUR ATTACKS MIGHT NOT DO ANYTHING TO THEM.
BUT I'M SURE WE CAN DISTRACT THEM LONG ENOUGH FOR YOU TO HAVE TIME TO BLAST THEM ALL.
I'M STARTING TO SENSE SOMETHING...
TO BE HONEST, I WAS VERY SKEPTICAL OF THIS RUDIMENTARY PLAN BY YOUR HUMAN FRIEND—
BUT THIS IS BETTER THAN NOTHING.
COME ALONG, NOW!
WAIT, WHAT? WAIT UP! GUYS, FOLLOW THE CAT!
WHOOOSH
THAT'S IT? THAT'S JUST A TINY LEAK.
WHAT ARE WE LOOKING AT?
THERE'S MORE UP AHEAD. QUICKLY NOW, YOU MUST TRANSFORM.

YOU DON'T SEE THE LEAK?
UH... WELL...
LOOKS LIKE A REGULAR CRACK IN THE PAVEMENT.
AS YOU SAID, THIS IS A SMALL ONE. YOUR HUMAN FRIEND CANNOT DETECT THE SIGNIFICANCE OF IT.
AHHHH!
SPHHHA
AHHH, MY EYES!
HYAH!
SMACK
YOU OKAY?! WHAT KIND OF SPRAY WAS THAT?
BUG SPRAY.
HEHEHE, NICE.
TWITCH
TWITCH
AHHH!
IT'S STILL ALIVE!

HEY, MAX, I THINK NOW'S A GOOD TIME TO TRANSFORM INTO MAGICAL BOY!
R-RIGHT!
BUT WHAT IF IT DOESN'T WORK?
LIKE MOM SAID, MY WAY IS UNRELIABLE...
WHAT IF I CAN'T PROTECT THEM?
PAT
HEY.
IT'S OKAY, MAX. WE'RE ALL HERE FOR YOU.
YEAH, MAX. YOU GOT THIS IN THE BAG!
THIS IS A LITTLE BIT FRIGHTENING, BUT DON'T LET THAT STOP YOU.
IT WON'T STOP ME. IT'S PAYBACK TIME.
THANKS, GUYS.

RIGHT.
WHO CARES WHAT MY MOM SAYS.
INHALE
I MAY STRUGGLE, BUT I'VE GOT WHAT IT TAKES TO DO THIS...
OH NO! IT'S THE DESCENDANT OF AURORA!
HISSS
AS MYSELF!
HYAHH!
WHOOSHH
THIS IS IT! THIS IS MAGICAL BOY!
YAASS! BOI, YOU DID IT!

WHOOSH
BING
BING
SNATCH
ZAP
ZAP
ZAP
STAB
WHOOOSH
NOT BAD. IT SEEMS YOU'RE GETTING USED TO YOUR POWERS, DESPITE YOUR...METHODS.
THEY MAY BE DRASTICALLY DIFFERENT FROM THE WAYS OF YOUR ANCESTORS, BUT IF IT WORKS, I HAVE NO QUARREL WITH IT.
COME NOW, THERE'S MORE TO BE DONE.

SMACK
SPHHH
WHACK
ZAP
ZAP
ZAP
STAB
WHOOOSH
THAT'S NOT NORMAL.
THAT HAS TO BE IT, RIGHT?
LET'S GO.

Episode 15:
WITHIN THE FOREST

YEAH, THAT HAS TO BE A GATE.
HMMM. IT IS QUITE A BIT LARGER THAN THE OTHERS, BUT SOMETHING'S OFF.
HAHA! AT THIS RATE, I'LL BECOME GATEKEEPER OF THE THIRD GATE!
STOMP
STOMP
YOU!
!
OH, LOOK AT WHAT WE HAVE HERE.
WAIT... ISN'T THAT THE SAME ONE FROM LAST TIME?
YEAH, WALNUT! WHAT THE HECK? HOW IS HE BACK?
I THOUGHT MAX KILLED THIS THING ALREADY!
DON'T BE ABSURD. YOU'RE NOT KILLING THEM WHEN YOU BLAST THEM WITH YOUR POWERS.

AURORA'S LIGHT PURIFIES THEM.
IT STRIPS THEM OF THEIR ILL-GAINED TOXIC POWERS...
AND FORCES THEM BACK TO THE OTHER REALM.
LOOKS LIKE THIS ONE GOT ALL ROTTEN AGAIN AND SNUCK ITS WAY BACK.
GUESS I'LL HAVE TO DO IT ALL OVER AGAIN!
WELL, THAT'S JUST FRUSTRATING!
ZAP!
YOU WON'T CATCH ME OFF GUARD THIS TIME!
WHOOSH
SWHOOOSH

THUNK
!
I WILL FINISH YOU THIS TIME!
!
NO YOU WON'T!
WHOOOM
ARGH!
WHAT ARE YOU FOOLS STANDING AROUND FOR?! DRAIN THESE HUMANS TO THEIR CORE!
AHHH!
STEP
STEP
OKAY, MAX, LEAVE THE SMALLER ONES TO US.
I'M SO GLAD THAT WORKED.
SNAP
WE'LL GIVE YOU AN OPENING FOR THE BIG GUY!

WHAM
SPHHHHH
WHOOSH
WHOOOSH
!
THUNK
YOUR FRIEND MAY HAVE COMPROMISED MY SIGHT, BUT I CAN STILL HEAR AND SMELL YOU.
SLAM
!
WHAM!
YOU'RE NOTHING LIKE YOUR PREDECESSORS. CLUMSY AND CARELESS.
YOU ARE WEAK.
GAK
DON'T FORGET ABOUT ME!
SLASH!
ARRGH!
MY OTHER ARM!

PUNT
YOU LITTLE...!
OH NO YOU DON'T!
BAM!
!
STOMP
YOU WERE A FOOL TO BRING THEM WITH YOU.
MAX!
I'M OUT OF BUG SPRAY!
I'M GONNA NEED A BIGGER PAN.
I'LL CRUSH ALL THE HOPE THEY HAVE FOR YOU AND USE THEIR TAINTED LIGHT TO POWER UP MY GATE. HAHAHA!
HOW DOES IT FEEL TO HAVE FAILED SO BADLY COMPARED TO THE OTHER GODDESSES?
ENDING YOU WILL GIVE ME NOT ONLY GREAT JOY, BUT ALSO THE MEANS TO RISE UP THE RANKS BY THE KING OF DARKNESS HIMSELF!
PRESS

SNAP
YOU TALK TOO MUCH!
SWOOSH
!
STAB
AHHHH!
FWOOP
BZZZ
WHOOSH
BZZ
BZZ
RAHHHH!
WHAT?!
BLOOP
NO, NO, NO, DON'T DO THIS TO ME NOW!
BAM
ACK!

ARE YOU ALL RIGHT?
YEAH, I'M OKAY...
...BUT MY STAFF—
IT'S OKAY. YOU'VE BEEN KICKING BUTT AND STAYING STRONG.
YEAH, YOUR STAFF PROBABLY JUST NEEDS TO BE BROKEN IN MORE.
SHAKE IT UP AND TRY AGAIN.
AGREED! DON'T GIVE UP YET! WE'RE JUST GETTING STARTED.
YOU GUYS.
I WILL NOT...
BE MADE A FOOL OF!

WAOOO
IT'S OVER, BUDDY.
FWOOSH
NOT AGAINNN!!
FWOOP
HAAA!
THUD
BOOOOM

AHH!
!
THEY'RE ALL GETTING SUCKED IN.
GOOD RIDDANCE.
BWEEOOOP
YAAAS! YOU DID IT, MAX!
WHOOOSH!
TING
THAT WAS SO EXCITING!
RUMBLE
!
WHAT?!
RUMBLE
RUMBLE
THIS DOESN'T MAKE SENSE! WE JUST CLOSED A GATE, DIDN'T WE?!
RUMBLE
RUMBLE
RUMBLE
PLEASE TELL ME THIS IS UNRELATED!
RUMBLE
!
OH, LOOK, YOUR CAT'S OKAY. THAT'S ONE TOUGH KITTY.
JUST AS I THOUGHT. THIS WAS SIMPLY A LARGE LEAK.

THE THIRD GATE...
...IS OPEN.
!!
I...
...FAILED.

UH...
DID THE CAT JUST...
TALK?
DON'T THE MISS THE THRILLING CONCLUSION IN
Magical Boy
VOL. 2!